MONKEY FLIP

Michael Dell

For Victoria Thompson, beloved mentor and friend, without whom the world would be short one talking-chimp book.

CHAPTER ONE

The boos started as soon as he walked through the curtain.

Three hundred rabid pro wrestling fans had packed the South Hadleyburg Fire Department Bingo Hall to witness this very moment. Yes, the entire card had been enjoyable—featuring the likes of Vince Manero, Mad Mike Dean, and women's champion Jill Johnson—but it had all built to this main event.

Bonecrusher Brannigan, a beefy mountain of a man, barreled to the ring in his signature black wrestling singlet, black boots, and black mask, a fearsome nightmare brought to life. He raved and roared at the combative crowd, swatting away their derisive jeers like imaginary biplanes. Bonecrusher towered over two children in the front row— a scrawny, bespectacled eleven-year-old boy with sensitive eyes and his pigtailed kid sister—and growled a ghastly threat that sent the little girl cowering into her brother's arms. The despicable display enraged the crowd anew, and the angry protests thundered within the same walls that hosted weekly spaghetti dinners, church fundraisers, and annual fish fries during Lent.

Bonecrusher climbed the ring apron and forced down the top rope so he could step over it like a true giant. He ran the length of the eighteen-foot squared circle and exploded into the ropes, slingshotting himself from one side to the other in a frightening display of speed and power. He reclaimed the center of the ring and raised a defiant fist. Who would be brave enough to answer the challenge? Who could possibly defeat this brutal behemoth?

The first note of the champion's theme song struck the air, and the boos magically transformed into gleeful cheers of excitement.

Mitch Mayhem, the reigning, defending Keystone Championship Wrestling Heavyweight Champion, emerged from the same curtained hallway that had unleashed Bonecrusher, although he did so with a decidedly different presence. Mitch walked to the ring with calm confidence, forsaking high-energy theatrics for cocky self-assuredness. A grizzled veteran of the independent scene, he had made this walk countless times, and that storied history was stitched on his weathered face, which bore the crow's feet and gray-stubbled beard of experience. His thinning black hair, once thick and full, was slicked straight back over exposed scalp, and the gold championship belt around his waist failed to distract from his skinny-fat physique that conveyed a complete lack of athleticism. Despite his advancing age and lack of muscle definition, Mitch opted to wear his customary baby blue wrestling trunks and red boots, the triangle of three white stars on the front of the trunks nearly as pale as his sagging flesh. Yet the fans still chanted his name and shouted encouragement, for he was their champion, their hero, their only hope to slay the beast that was Bonecrusher Brannigan.

The diminutive referee, who somehow still seemed more imposing than Mitch Mayhem, struggled to keep Bonecrusher at bay while the champion mounted the turnbuckles and acknowledged his adoring fans. Once every single ticket-buyer in attendance had feasted their eyes upon his greatness, Mitch strode confidently to the center of the ring, kissed his championship title, and handed it to the referee, who accepted it as if receiving the holiest of religious relics. A portly man in an ill-fitting blue tuxedo announced the combatants from a safe position at ringside, and the referee lifted the championship title above his head for all to see, making certain everyone knew the stakes.

At the sound of the bell, Bonecrusher bull-rushed the champion and drove him into the corner, where he unleashed a barrage of malicious forearm smashes and rib-splintering knees. The referee counted to five and then tried to intervene on Mitch's behalf, but a feigned backhand from Bonecrusher chased him away. After delivering a few more devastating knees to Mitch's midsection,

Bonecrusher captured his lifeless opponent by the wrist and whipped him into the far corner with enough force to shatter a cinderblock. The collision with the turnbuckles caused Mitch to stagger forward into a running tackle that nearly cut him in two, eliciting gasps from the crowd. Just when it seemed as though things couldn't get worse, Bonecrusher drew his thumb across his own throat, signaling that it was time for the Pulverizer, the most feared finishing move in all of Western Pennsylvania. Bonecrusher scooped Mitch off the mat and draped him belly-down on his right shoulder like a bar rag. He leapt high into the air and allowed all his weight to fall on Mitch in an earthquaking power slam. The referee slid into position to count the pin.

One.

Two.

Kickout!

Mitch kicked out! Bonecrusher couldn't believe it. He grabbed the referee by the collar and held up three fingers. The referee, trembling like a mouse in the clutches of a jungle cat, insisted that it was only a two count. When Bonecrusher finally quit berating the official, he turned to find an enraged Mitch ready to fight.

Bonecrusher lashed out with a right hand, but Mitch blocked it and countered with three stiff jabs, snapping Bonecrusher's head back. Wobbled, Bonecrusher fired a wild clothesline that missed its mark. Mitch sprang off the ropes and drove a jumping knee into Bonecrusher's spine. The challenger moaned and clutched his lower back. It was all the opening Mitch needed. He chopped Bonecrusher's legs with a rapid series of kicks, and like a determined lumberjack hacking into the trunk of a towering sequoia, he methodically chipped away until his foe toppled. Bonecrusher tried to secure his footing but ate another running knee that sent him crashing onto his back. Mitch pounced, trapping Bonecrusher's head and right arm in his patented mongoose vise, a crippling submission move from which there was no escape. Mitch wrenched on Bonecrusher's neck and shoulder with all his might. Bonecrusher howled in agony and tapped the mat with his free hand, begging for mercy. The referee called for the bell. There was much rejoicing.

Mitch Mayhem relinquished his hold and rose the conquering hero. He had done the impossible. He had tamed the monstrous Bonecrusher Brannigan.

While the fans showered their champion with praise, few noticed the defeated Bonecrusher rolling out of the ring. The ravenous beast who had raged his way to the ring just minutes earlier was now leaving a broken man, rubbing his sore neck and no doubt wondering where it all went wrong.

Mitch yanked his arm away from the referee and demanded the ring announcer's microphone. For someone who had just defended the KCW Heavyweight Championship in spectacular fashion, he appeared less than pleased.

"If you'll indulge me, I've got some things to get off my chest," Mitch said, that one simple statement turning the microphone into a lit stick of dynamite. Mitch's reputation had largely been built upon his ability on the mic, and his fans, already whipped into a frenzy, were eager to hear another legendary promo. "There's been a lot of rumors going around online about me and Mad Mike Dean, isn't that right, Steve?" He directed his question to a humorless man in the front row with cropped salt-and-pepper hair and a face like boiled cauliflower. "There he is, everybody, the famous *wrasslin'* journalist Steve Thacker. He gets all the scoops, even if he has to make them up. No story is too flimsy, no lie too large. All about those clicks. Ain't that right, Steve?"

If offended by Mitch's insults, Thacker certainly didn't show it. He sat quietly, hands folded, displaying all the emotion of dry toast.

"Sure, Mad Mike and I used to be tag team partners. Had a heck of a run. Won some titles. Even won some of good ol' Steve's awards. But I haven't had anything to do with Mad Mike Dean for over five years. Wanted nothing to do with him even longer than that. It's unfortunate that I have to talk about this when I should be celebrating another title defense. If I decide not to be friends with someone, it's nobody else's business. But my problem was I wanted to bring a guy with me to the top who didn't want to see me succeed. Call it jealousy, call it envy, whatever. My relationship with Mad Mike Dean is over. Dead. I do not talk to Mad Mike Dean. I do not even want to look at Mad Mike Dean. And I will certainly never wrestle Mad Mike Dean. Let it go. And, Steve, I know who gives you all your info, and you can tell your pal Manero I think he's a stooge too."

Mitch's fans delighted in the dirty laundry being aired publicly and voiced their approval, but at least one member of the crowd was entirely uninterested. The little girl in pigtails who Bonecrusher had terrorized on his way to the ring pulled her older brother with her and sneaked up the main aisle to the entrance curtain. No one paid them any mind. All eyes were on the ring. Mitch had everyone eating out of the palm of his hand, and he had more to say.

"Now, on to more important things. What did I ever do to deserve an empty-headed loser like Lenny Lambda to come out here in front of the best fans in wrestling and go into business for himself? For what? To embarrass me? What did I ever do to deserve that? And when somebody who hasn't done anything in this business jeopardizes my money and my name, it's a disgrace to this company, a disgrace to this industry. We're far beyond apologies. I gave him a chance, and it didn't get handled. So now, here we are. And this goes to everyone in the back, if you have a problem with me, do something about it."

The brother and sister duo slipped through the entrance curtain, which was actually just two flannel blankets duct taped to the walls, and entered the secret realm of professional wrestlers. Mitch's tirade against his co-workers continued, and the crowd's vocal support for his diatribe reverberated throughout the backstage hall that led to the various offices and supply closets that served as dressing rooms during wrestling events. The kids peeked around the corner of one such makeshift dressing room and found Bonecrusher Brannigan sitting alone, slowly unraveling black athletic tape from his wrists. Normally reserved for important bingo hall business meetings, on this night, the room had its table—which boasted some stray pens and markers for autograph seekers, a coffee machine, bottles of water, and the remnants of a picked-over pastry tray—shoved against the far wall to make space for a semi-circle of metal folding chairs that served as changing stations, just one of the many perks of being an independent wrestler. Bonecrusher balled up the used tape and dropped it into the gear bag between his feet. Gone was the crazed berserker who could smash worlds with his bare hands. He was just a man—a beaten, broken, humbled man.

The little girl walked right up to the formidable Bonecrusher. "What the heck was that?"

"Oh, hey, guys." Bonecrusher pulled off his mask, revealing a broad, friendly face. His large blue eyes were far softer than his somewhat generous midsection and twinkled with a warmth found in only the gentlest of souls or the truly stupid. "I thought it went pretty good."

"Are you kidding me?" the little girl said. "He buried you."

Bonecrusher pushed his hand through his short, sweat-matted blond hair, causing it to stand up in stray tufts and making him look like a balding hedgehog. "I don't know about that. I mean, he gave me a lot of offense early. Even let me hit my finisher."

"Yeah, so he could kick out of it." She paced back and forth in front of Bonecrusher like a miniature military strategist waging a losing war. "The Pulverizer's dead. Forget about it ever being taken seriously as a finisher again. And you're supposed to be a monster heel, but he made you tap out. You quit! No coming back from that. Guess we're in the mid-card again, if we're lucky. We'll probably be doing jobs every weekend now." She stopped in front of Bonecrusher and threw her hands in the air. "How could you let him do that to you?"

Bonecrusher looked to the little boy, who had been silently lingering on the edge of the room. "What do you think, Benny? Was it really that bad?"

"Addie tends to be a bit dramatic."

His sister cocked her fist. "Bennett, you tell Daddy the truth right now, or so help me…."

Bennett studied the tops of his shoes for a way out. "It wasn't the best."

"Thank you!" Addie said.

Their father's broad shoulders collapsed beneath the shame. He looked once more to Addie. "Was it really that bad?"

"The worst."

"Good thing your mother wasn't here to see it. But, hey, you guys were great when I made my entrance. Got good heat from the crowd."

"Of course it did," Addie said. "We're professionals. Which is more than I can say for Mitch. He had to know what that match was gonna do to you. What did he say when you were going over things?"

"Just to start hot and then he'd call it in the ring."

Addie smacked herself in the forehead. "Not only did you get buried, you gave him the shovel."

"What was I supposed to do?"

"You could have stood up for yourself."

"But it's Mitch. He's the champ. I was lucky to even be working with him."

"What kind of attitude is that? If you want to be champ, you've got to—"

The sound of Mitch's music interrupted Addie's pep talk, signaling that the champion was leaving the ring. "He didn't change in here, did he?"

"No, he has his own room."

"Good. Because if he came in here, I'd sock him in the eye."

They heard Mitch's music get louder when the curtain opened, followed by the pounding of determined footsteps. The champion, his glistening gold title adorning his shoulder, streaked by on his way down the hall.

"He doesn't even thank you for the match?" Addie said.

Her dad started unlacing his boots. "He's a busy guy."

"Yet he always has time to be a jerk."

They heard a door slam and Mitch shout, "Tony!" More angry stomping. A frantic Mitch reappeared in the doorway and scanned the room, the dark circles under his eyes making him look like a demented raccoon in search of his next garbage can. "You seen Tony?"

Addie and Bennett's father snapped to attention. "No, sorry. But thanks for the match. Was an honor to share the ring with you."

"Yeah, whatever. If you see Tony, tell him I'm looking for hi— ooh, are those muffins?" Mitch tramped past Addie, Bennett, and their father on his way to the refreshments. He dropped his championship on the table and glommed the one remaining blueberry muffin. "I'm starving. Haven't eaten since dinner."

"Hey!"

Mitch, muffin crumbs clinging to the corner of his mouth, turned to find Addie at his hip. "You talkin' to me?"

"Yeah, I'm talking to you. What gives with you treating Daddy like that?"

Mitch looked to Bonecrusher with arrogant disdain. "This your kid?"

"Sorry, Mitch," her dad said, hurrying over to defuse the situation. "She's a big fan, really."

"You haven't smartened her up?"

"I'm not a mark, dummy," Addie said. "I know you weren't really fighting. But why'd you have to bury him?"

"What are you talking about?" Mitch said with a mouthful of muffin. "I didn't—"

"Here he is!" called a voice from the doorway.

The man who shouted the alert was Ricky Hickson, one half of the KCW Tag Team Champions, the Hickson Brothers. He was almost immediately joined by his older brother Ronnie, who pointed at Mitch and waved frantically to an unseen individual down the hall. The two brothers had a clear family resemblance, both sporting long brown hair past their shoulders and enough scruff on their cheeks to almost count as beards. Neither was particularly intimidating, and their absurd wardrobes—some bizarre tribute to 1970s fashion disasters, complete with matching silk shirts, flared jeans, and platform shoes that still left them shy of the average height for a grown adult human—made them all the more laughable as supposed wrestlers. While the brothers were two years apart in age, the only real way to tell one from the other was that Ricky had a pie face worthy of Sara Lee, and Ronnie's hairline was receding faster than a cheetah on roller skates.

A third man raided the room and made a beeline for Mitch. This was Lenny Lambda, the darling of the internet wrestling community. Famous for his fast-paced matches and high-flying maneuvers, Lambda had received more five-star ratings from Steve Thacker than any wrestler in history, and he even reached seven stars, which is quite the achievement when rated on a five-star scale. Lambda's black leather pants restricted his gait to a stiff-legged shuffle, but unlike Mitch and the Hickson Brothers, he at least looked athletic, and his upper body showed some muscle tone beneath a light blue Final Fantasy T-shirt. He removed his imitation Ray-Ban sunglasses and stared at Mitch through the curly frosted tips of his shaggy mullet. "Heard you've been talking about me."

"Good," Mitch said, still munching muffin. "That was the point."

"Why don't you try saying it to my face?"

"Yeah, say it to his face," Ronnie Hickson said, he and his brother hopping up and down on either side of Lambda like excitable elves.

Addie and Bennett's father tried to intervene. "Maybe we should all just calm down and take a—"

"Stay out of it, Crusher," Lambda said in his trademarked tough-guy voice. "This is between me and the old man here."

"Yeah, between him and the old man," Ronnie Hickson said.

Mitch didn't appear threatened in the least. He took his time chewing the last of his muffin, meeting Lambda's death stare with wry amusement. Bonecrusher's paternal instincts kicked in.

"Bennett, take your sister out into the hallway please."

"No way," Addie said. "I want to see this."

Mitch swallowed the last of his muffin, cleared his throat, and smiled at Lambda. "You're an empty-headed loser and a disgrace to the industry."

The Hickson Brothers were outraged at the disrespect and flopped about like two guppies free of their fishbowl. "You're gonna get it now, old man," Ronnie Hickson said.

"Yeah, you're gonna get it now," echoed his brother.

Lambda was so furious that he put his sunglasses back on just so he could rip them off again. "What did you say?"

"You heard me," Mitch said.

"Say it again. I dare you."

"Addie, seriously," her dad said, "go out in the hall with your brother."

"Aw, man. I miss all the good stuff."

"Here they are," Tony Katsaros, the KCW owner and promoter, said, mincing into the room like a prize-winning pony. Tony's curly black hair bounced with each prancing step, and his manic behavior, unshaven face, and googly-eyed expression made him seem like a mascot for paranoia. His baggy purple tracksuit was in stark contrast to the tailored business attire of the two women trailing behind him, the younger of whom carried a tablet device and seemed to be taking notes.

Lambda turned to see the new arrivals, and Mitch took full advantage, punching him in the side of the head. The surprise left hook had all the power of a broken light switch, and Lambda and the Hickson Brothers quickly retaliated in a fury of fitful slaps and hair pulling. Tony shrieked and ducked behind the two businesswomen, who were aghast at the uncivilized outburst. While Bennett retreated to the safety of the refreshment table with Addie, their father waded into the melee and tried to break it up, but his girth only added to the chaos. All four participants and the one misguided peacemaker became entangled and fell to the floor, where they rolled about kicking and screaming like a preschool class in need of a nap.

Meanwhile, even though Bennett clung to her waist to prevent her from joining the fight, Addie lashed out with her little limbs in hopes of hitting anyone who got too close. "Get 'em, Daddy! Work the leg! Work the leg!"

The older of the two businesswomen said, "Mr. Katsaros, I think we've seen enough." She squired her young colleague from the room.

Tony chased them as far as the door and called out, "Thanks for coming, Ms. Stanwick. We'll talk soon, okay? Ms. Stanwick?"

Addie and Bennett's father flung the Hickson Brothers aside and then stood between Mitch and Lambda, who both seemed ready for a breather. "Enough! My kids are in here. What kind of an example are we setting?"

"A pretty bad one," Addie said, still swinging haymakers at no one in particular. "None of you clowns know how to punch."

Lambda, the neck of his T-shirt stretched beyond repair, touched his scalp for any signs of blood. "He started it."

"Give me a second to catch my breath," Mitch said, "and I'll finish it."

Tony stamped his foot, although it generated about as much noise as a feather falling on cotton. "Do you guys have any idea what you just did? Those ladies were with the network. We were gonna be on Saturday nights at one-thirty, which everyone knows is huge for our demo, and you probably ruined it. What do you have to say for yourselves?" He stood hands on hips, his suede loafer beating a nervous rhythm on the cheap carpeting. "Well? I'm waiting."

Mitch smoothed his hair back into place. "I'd say I'm the only reason they were here to begin with, and you should probably think twice before talking to me like that."

Tony's face went chalk white. "I'm sure I'll be able to work things out with the network. How are you feeling? Hope you weren't hurt in that little dustup. Can I get you something? Cup of coffee? Donut? Cash?"

"I'm sick of you always taking his side," Lambda said.

"Yeah," Ronnie Hickson said, "Lenny's sick of it."

Tony forced a laugh. "We're all on the same team here. There aren't any *sides*."

Mitch fixed Tony with cruel contempt. "Yes, there are. And you're either with me or against me."

Tony latched onto Mitch with a painfully awkward hug, the likes of which are seldom seen outside of lovesick koalas. "Oh, I'm with you, Mitch. Don't you worry about that. Team Mitch, that's what I always say."

"What's he got that I don't got?" Lambda said. "I should be on top. I'm the future."

"That may be true, kid," Mitch said. "But I ain't done with the present yet. Get in line."

"You're seriously going to pick him over me?"

Tony reluctantly disengaged from his cherished champion. "Mitch is a needle mover. He's a star. And it's up to all of us to treat him as such. The brighter he shines, the better we look." Tony shooed Lambda and the Hickson Brothers out of the way. "Let me walk you to your car, Mitch. We can kick around ideas for your next program."

Mitch stopped at the door. "My title."

"Let me get it," Tony said.

Addie clicked a marker cap shut. "Don't worry, Tiny. I got it." She pitched the marker on the refreshment table and dutifully carried the gold-plated, white-leather belt to its owner. "Here ya go, Mitch."

The champ accepted it without thanks.

"Uh, Addie?" Tony said.

"Yeah?"

"My name's Tony."

"What did I say?"

"Tiny."

"I did? My bad."

"Just remember it's Tony, like the tiger." He made his hands into claws. "Growwwl."

"Yeah, yeah. Like the tiger. No problem."

Tony returned to fawning over Mitch. "Let's go, champ."

Mitch raised the title belt high above his head. "Hey, Lenny. Get a good look. You're never gonna have this as long as I'm around."

With that, he turned and headed down the hall, Tony's hyperactive chatter providing the soundtrack for his departure.

Lambda and the Hickson Brothers looked back at Addie and Bennett's dad before they made their exits.

"You're gonna have to pick a side, Crusher," Lambda said. "Choose wisely." He punctuated the closing statement by putting on his sunglasses, but the frames had been damaged in the scuffle and sat cockeyed on his face. "Lambda out."

Both Hickson Brothers pointed menacingly at them in a final warning before running after Lambda, their platform shoes pitter-pattering the hallway.

While they watched their dad gather his belongings, Bennett whispered to Addie, "What were you doing with that marker?"

"Just left a little message for Mitch on the inside of the belt."

"You shouldn't destroy property like that."

"Who destroyed property? I just made sure everyone will know the belt belongs to him."

Bonecrusher zipped up his bag, the weight of the night's events sagging his meaty shoulders. "Okay, guys," he said. "Let's go home."

Addie, Bennett, and their father made the walk to the car in silence. Bonecrusher was so distracted by the night's events, he didn't even bother to change out of his wrestling gear. On the way home, he tried to lighten the mood, suggesting they see who could name the most WWE Intercontinental Champions. He started things off with Tito Santana, and then Bennett, who had allowed his sister to ride shotgun, chimed in with the Honky Tonk Man from the back seat.

"Your turn, Addie," their father said.

But Addie remained silent, simply staring straight ahead, her arms crossed and a sour expression on her face.

"Addie? You okay?"

"No, I'm not okay."

"I told you not to eat so many Swedish Fish," Bennett said.

"It's not the fish, dummy," Addie said. "It's Mitch." She shifted in the seat to look at her dad. "You can't let him push you around like that."

"You heard Tony," her dad said, keeping his eyes on the road. "Mitch is a star. I can't rock the boat."

"He buried you tonight. He embarrassed you."

"I didn't feel embarrassed."

"*I* was embarrassed for you. It was humiliating. Wasn't it, Bennett?"

Her brother adjusted his glasses. "Well, I—"

"See, Bennett agrees with me. You have to do something. If you don't stand up to Mitch now, you're going to be taking it the rest of your career."

"But Tony said we—"

"Who cares what Tiny says? He's scared of his own shadow. The room needs a leader."

"Okay, but why does it have to be me?"

"Because you respect the business. And you know what Mitch is doing is wrong. You know it deep down in your guts. Am I right or am I right?"

Their father contemplated the question a moment, the only sound in the car being the clicking of a turn signal. "You're right."

"Was there ever any doubt? You're one of the few people in the company Mitch doesn't hate, so he might actually listen to you. Plus, you're way bigger than him and could smoosh him like a bug."

Their dad pulled the car into the driveway of their modest ranch-style home and left the engine running.

"Yeah, who does he think he is pushing me around? I'm every bit the worker he is."

"Better even."

"I deserve respect. I should be champ, not him."

"That's the spirit."

"I'm gonna go settle this right now."

Addie reattached her seatbelt. "Let's roll."

"No, I need to do this alone. Man to man."

Bennett leaned forward from the back seat. "Are you sure you want to do this?"

"Of course he's sure," Addie said. "If he doesn't, who will? You're Bonecrusher Brannigan. You fear no man. Now go give Mitch a piece of your mind. Show him what's up. And don't take no for an answer. Got it?"

"Got it." He curled his upper lip into a snarl and stared at his powerful hands strangling the steering wheel. But before Addie and Bennett fully exited the car, his stone face softened. "Hey, don't forget to tell Mommy where I am and that I'll be home late. Wouldn't want to make her mad."

Addie and Bennett stood silently beneath the moonlit sky and watched their dad drive off toward destiny.

"Think he's really gonna do it?" Bennett asked.

Addie shrugged and went inside.

Their mother was sitting propped up in the corner of the living room couch, a law textbook resting against her bent knees and a pencil tucked behind her ear. A petite brunette, she barely occupied one couch cushion, and her baggy sweatshirt and plaid pajama pants made her seem even tinier, like an orphan waiting to grow into hand-me-downs. So engrossed in her studies, she didn't bother to look up when she heard the door open. "How'd it go?"

Addie plopped down on the middle couch cushion. "Daddy got buried."

"That'll happen."

"Mitch gave him nothing. Kicked out of the Pulverizer and everything."

"You'll get him next time." But when their mother finally did pry herself away from the paralegal profession, Bennett had already shut the door and was taking off his shoes. There was no sign of her husband. "Where's your father?"

"He went to go talk to Mitch," Bennett said.

"Yeah, he's finally gonna stand up for himself," Addie said.

Their mother laughed. "I'll believe that when I see it."

"No, I think he's really going to do it this time," Bennett said.

"I gave him a good talking to," Addie said, picking at some loose strands of the frayed couch cushion. "Mitch did him wrong, and Daddy's gonna set him straight. Nobody buries Bonecrusher Brannigan and gets away with it."

"I'm sure you'll hear all about it tomorrow," their mother said. "Go brush your teeth and get ready for bed. I'll be back to tuck you in after I finish this chapter."

"How do you expect me to sleep when Daddy's career could be over?"

Their mother lowered her textbook. "Your father is a mechanic. Wrestling isn't a career. It's just a dumb hobby that he should have given up by now. Most adults grow out of it, and I'm really hoping it happens to the two of you sooner rather than later. Now, please go get ready for bed. And, Bennett, make sure she brushes her teeth." She fixed her daughter with a disappointed stare. "I don't want to just hear the water turn on and you scrubbing the sink."

"Fine. But is it any wonder Daddy isn't champion with that attitude? Hope you're real proud of yourself."

"I'll do my best to live with the shame." She gave Addie a playful swat on the bottom with her notebook. "Get."

Addie sold the blow like buckshot. "Do you see how she treats me?"

"C'mon," Bennett said. He led his little sister to their waiting toothbrushes. They would both go to sleep not knowing whether the mighty Bonecrusher Brannigan got even with the dastardly Mitch Mayhem. But in Addie's dreams, he most certainly did.

CHAPTER TWO

The next morning, Bennett was the first to wake up, as was customary. Being that it was a Sunday in June, he could have easily slept in well past seven, but he enjoyed sticking to a regimented schedule. It built discipline. He pulled on his gold terrycloth robe, stepped into his slippers, and headed to the kitchen for a nutritious breakfast of dry bran cereal and water. If he avoided making too much noise, he could probably have the TV to himself for an hour or so before Addie woke up. But when he reached the end of the hall, he confronted a most unusual sight: his father was sound asleep on the living room couch and still wearing his wrestling gear. Before Bennett could make sense of the situation, he heard Addie stumbling out of her bedroom and hurrying down the hall.

"Oh, no you don't," she said, still rubbing the sleep from her eyes. "I get the TV first. You can wait until—"

Like her brother before her, Addie was also dumbstruck at seeing her father passed out on the couch, his arms and legs splayed wide, his prominent belly rising and falling like that of a drunken bear.

"Think they're fighting again?" Bennett asked.

"Probably." Addie yawned. "Should we wake him?"

"Maybe we should let him sleep. He looks tired, and he can get grouchy when he's tired."

"But I want to know what happened with Mitch."

"He'll tell us when he gets up."

"That could be hours. And I want to watch TV." She elbowed her brother. "Wake him up."

"You do it."

"You're older."

"How come that only matters when it's something you don't want to do?"

"Don't be a baby."

"I'm not a baby."

"Are to."

"Am not."

"That's exactly what a baby would say."

Neither of the squabbling siblings noticed their mother until she barged between them and gave the couch a contentious kick. "Hey!"

Their father startled awake. "Huh, what's wrong? What—oh, hi, honey."

"Don't honey me," their mother said, her face almost as red as her pajama pants. "Where were you all night?"

"Got home late from Mitch's and was still a bit wired. Just wanted to unwind a minute before going to bed. Guess I dozed off."

"Scared me when I woke up and you weren't there."

"Sorry. Didn't mean to—"

"Yeah, yeah." Their mother turned and headed to the kitchen. "And change your clothes already. You look ridiculous."

Addie jumped on the couch next to her dad. "How'd it go with Mitch? Did you have to rough him up?"

"No, it actually went really well. Said he respected me for coming to talk to him. He even apologized."

"That doesn't sound like Mitch," Bennett said.

"I hear ya. But I think it was sincere. He really does love the business. Told some great stories about his early days on the road. And he promised to bury the hatchet with Lambda and the Hicksons."

"Wow, you may have saved the company."

"You know what, Benny? I think you're right."

"You deserve a Pop Tart," Addie said.

"Make it two."

"You got it, Crusher. Need to keep your weight up if you're gonna make a serious title run."

"Let's not get ahead of ourselves. I still have a ways to go before I'm the—"

A loud knock at the front door interrupted the thought.

"Who's that?" their mother said from the kitchen.

"Don't know." Their father forced himself up from the couch and stretched his aching back. "Go help your mother with breakfast. I'll see who it is."

While Addie and Bennett went to retrieve the celebratory Pop Tarts, their father opened the front door to discover two uniformed police officers. Unsure exactly what to make of the situation, he carefully pushed open the glass storm door and said, "Can I help you, officers?"

"Stanley Pajakowski?"

"Yeah."

"Do you know a Mitch Alberts? He wrestles under the name Mitch Mayhem."

"Sure. I work with him."

"And when was the last time you saw Mr. Alberts?"

The rest of the family drifted in from the kitchen. Addie and Bennett's mother asked, "What's going on?"

"Mr. Pajakowski," the officer said, "maybe it would be best if you took a ride with us to the station so we can finish our conversation in private."

"Yeah, I guess I could—"

"My husband isn't going anywhere until you tell us what this is about."

"Ma'am, it's Mitch Alberts. He's been murdered."

CHAPTER THREE

On an idyllic June morning, the Pajakowski family car pulled in front of a majestic Victorian home, which seemed somewhat out of place in the surrounding neighborhood. While there were other similarly sized houses on the street, and they all shared the same gray or drab-colored exteriors, this particular home was the only one whose front porch spindles were ribboned in pastel pink and violet. The occupants of the car were familiar with the home, although the driver—Michelle Pajakowski—was far less enthusiastic about the owner's decorative flair than Addie and Bennett, who thought their grandmother's porch was pretty cool…for an old lady.

"Okay, now you guys be good for NiNi," their mother said. "And don't let her get you into any trouble."

"Why do you always say that?" Addie asked from the back seat. She was dressed in her Pioneer Scout uniform, complete with white shirt, green skirt, and matching green sash dotted with achievement badges.

"Because I know her better than you do. Bennett, you're in charge of the cookies. Please make sure that your sister sells more than she eats."

Bennett claimed the handles of the cookie-filled shopping bag, proudly accepting the added responsibility.

Their mother checked her lipstick in the sun visor's mirror. "And you got your backpacks and your phones?" She heard confirmation and flipped up the visor. "Listen, I know the past week has been really hard on you guys, what with Daddy being arrested and all. But I just want you to know that no matter what, we're a family, and families stick together. The three of us will get through this."

"The four of us," Addie said.

"What?"

"You said three. But there's four of us. You forgot Daddy."

"Oh, yeah, yeah. Daddy too."

"You know he didn't do it, right?" Bennett said.

Their mother took way too much time to respond. "Sure."

"He didn't do it," Addie said.

"Of course not. I definitely think it's possible that your father probably didn't murder Mitch. Maybe. But—and this is the important thing—he loves you both very much and would never hurt you. I mean, think of all the times he could have murdered us in our sleep, yet we're still here. That should tell you something." She glanced at the dashboard clock. "Shoot, I'm gonna be late. Have fun with NiNi. Sell lots of cookies. And I'll see you guys tonight, okay? Love you." She kissed both kids on the head and deposited them on the sidewalk outside their grandmother's house. The brother-and-sister duo watched their mother speed off, and they offered half-hearted waves goodbye until the car turned the corner and disappeared from view.

Bennett hefted the shopping bag full of Pioneer Scout cookies and turned to mount the front porch steps, only to have Addie drag him behind the row of hedges that marked their grandmother's property.

"Hey, knock it off," Bennett said. "I could have twisted my ankle."

"Shut it." Addie pulled her cell phone from her skirt pocket and dialed a number. "Hey, NiNi. Change of plans. Mommy is dropping us off at Jenny's house, and we're gonna sell cookies with her and her mom. Yeah, I know. We will. I'll call if we need a ride. Yep. Deuces."

As soon as the call disconnected, Bennett, his eyes wide with horror, said, "You lied to NiNi."

"Aw, calm down. She's a crazy old lady and will never know the difference. Besides, we got more important things to worry about."

"Like what?"

"Saving Daddy." Addie turned and started marching down the street.

Bennett trotted after her, the weight of his backpack and the cookie bag slowing his progress. "And how are we supposed to do that?"

"We're going to hire a detective."

"We don't know any detectives."

"You don't. I do."

"You're not making any sense. Hold up." Bennett cut in front of his sister to block her path and rested the cookie bag on the ground. "Where are you going?"

"Remember a few years ago when they were building that big fancy house at the top of Mulberry Hill? Tommy Wilkins says that the world's greatest detective lives there, but he's retired and keeps to himself. Never goes outside."

"How would Tommy Wilkins know that?"

"He knows things."

"Since when?"

"Since as long as I can remember. He's the one who told me about the buried treasure under the school playground."

"What buried treasure?"

"The one left behind by the space goats. Don't you know anything?"

Bennett placed his hands on his sister's shoulders. "Addie, there's no such thing as space goats. There is no treasure beneath the school playground. And I highly doubt the world's greatest detective lives in Hadleyburg, Pennsylvania. Let's go to NiNi's. We can say Jenny got sick and—"

Addie shook free from her brother. "Don't you get it? Everyone thinks Daddy did it. The police think he did it. Even Mommy thinks he did it. If we don't do something, he's gonna go to prison forever. But if we can convince this detective guy to take the case, we can find the real killer. It's up to us. No one else is gonna do it."

"I doubt a detective lives in that house."

"But we have to try, don't we?" She wiped away the early indications of a tear. "We're his only hope."

Bennett stared at his sister for a long moment, no doubt calculating the probabilities of success and then convincing himself to ignore the results. After considerable deliberation, he picked up the cookie bag in one hand and clasped his sister's hand in the other.

"C'mon. Mulberry Hill is a long walk. But if a detective does live there, please don't mention anything about the space goats."

"Good thinking," Addie said. "More treasure for us."

CHAPTER FOUR

Addie and Bennett needed nearly thirty minutes to reach the foot of Mulberry Hill. Their journey started from their grandmother's South Hadleyburg neighborhood and passed through the city's downtown business district, which featured more vacant storefronts than businesses. Along the way, they saw the City Hall, where their father currently resided behind bars, and the Court House, where his impending trial would be held. That knowledge served as extra motivation to continue their mission. The entire time, Bennett made certain that they crossed intersections within the crosswalks and obeyed all traffic signals. He also refused to let Addie help him carry the cookie bag—the cookies were his responsibility and his alone.

Mulberry Hill, so named due to the mulberry trees that lined the one winding roadway to its top, had once been the home of a liberal arts college, but the institution shuttered its doors when the administration decided that the only way to prove their virtuousness was to willingly cancel themselves before committing any future microaggressions. After the campus was demolished and the earth salted, the land sat untouched until a mysterious investor purchased the neglected property and began construction on a monumental private residence. The project was completed under the utmost secrecy, so perhaps the world's greatest detective actually did live there. Why this wealthy individual would forsake such exotic locales as the French Riviera or the Swiss Alps for a dreary little town in Western Pennsylvania seemed beyond comprehension, but that was of little concern to Addie and Bennett. They only cared that the detective was indeed at the top of the daunting hill that rose before them, and they were determined to make the climb one small step after another until they reached their goal.

Fifteen minutes later, they did just that, entering a circular driveway that coiled around a patch of overgrown grass in need of mowing. A fountain, which surely must have been impressive when operational due to its towering five-tiered spire, sat silent, its basin bone-dry. The questionable condition of the surrounding yard, with its unpruned shrubs and rampant weeds, did little to detract from the stupendous home itself, a sprawling, three-story colonial mansion that was ten times bigger than even their NiNi's house. Giant white columns supported a balustraded balcony above the front entrance, and a similar balcony could be seen extending from the right side of the home, providing additional shade for the wraparound porch beneath. There were more windows than in most of the office buildings downtown, although they were all heavily curtained, and at least four brick chimneys poked through the gabled roof. However, by far, the most distinctive feature of the home was its yellow exterior walls, which when combined with the ivory columns, railings, and cornices, created the impression of a lemon meringue pie thawing in the summer sun.

Bennett soaked in the unique visual. "What kind of a detective has a yellow house?"

"The kind that's gonna prove Daddy's innocent. C'mon." Addie led her brother up the granite steps of the front porch. "And remember, this guy doesn't like people, and he's supposedly retired, so we can't ask him to take Daddy's case right away. We're just here to sell cookies. Gotta play it cool. I know that's gonna be hard for you since you're not cool and probably never will be, but do what you can."

Addie pressed the doorbell. "Did you hear anything?"

Bennett shook his head.

"Maybe it's broken." She tried again, harder this time. Still nothing. "Work already, will ya?" She tapped the doorbell over and over, her finger stabbing the button like the beak of a persistent woodpecker.

"Stop it!"

Addie looked at Bennett.

"Wasn't me," he said.

She was about to resume her assault on the doorbell when the mysterious voice asked, "Who sent you? The government?"

Addie and Bennett looked around, still unable to detect the speaker's location.

"Uh, the Pioneer Scouts," Addie said to no one in particular.

"And you're here to offer your services to the revolution? Splendid. Can never have too many soldiers for the cause."

"Actually," Addie held up a box of snickerdoodles, "we're here to sell cookies. The money goes to support our troop's scouting activities and the local food bank."

"Likely story. I know a political shell game when I see one. Good luck pulling this nonsense after the revolution."

Bennett whispered, "Maybe we should go. He sounds a little crazy."

"Crazy?" said the voice. "Is it crazy to want a world based on truth, integrity, and moral fortitude? A world free of corruption and deceit, where peace, love, and empathy reign supreme. The powers that be divide society along ethnic, racial, and economic lines, destroying unity and brotherhood and intentionally obscuring the oneness of all creation simply to retain control. Or perhaps they worship something far more nefarious than their own egos? But that's a dark, disturbing rabbit hole few should explore, for it will leave you forever changed. The scales have fallen from my eyes, and I have seen the truth. And once seen, it cannot be ignored. If that makes me crazy, young man, then I do not wish to be sane."

"Anyway," Addie said, "we've got four varieties. Snickerdoodle."

"Yuck."

"Chocolate mint."

"Disgusting."

"Oatmeal."

"It keeps getting worse."

"And banana cream."

A loud *click* sounded, followed closely by two *clanks* and a *thunk*. The front door swung open, but there was still no one there, just a darkened doorway leading to an inky abyss. "Take the staircase up to the second floor, turn right, and I am in the third room on the left. Rest assured, you will be on camera the entire time, and if you stray from the prescribed route, I will have no choice but to release the hounds."

Addie shrugged and stepped over the threshold, but Bennett pulled her back outside. "What are you doing? NiNi told us never to go into a stranger's house. He could be an ax murderer or something."

Addie shouted into the yawning entranceway, "Hey, mister, are you an ax murderer?"

"I would never use an ax to murder you. Far too messy. A poisoned blow dart would be neater and much more efficient."

"See," Addie said to her brother.

"We shouldn't go in there."

"Oh, I'm sorry. I thought you loved Daddy. But that's okay. We can just tell him you were too scared to help the next time we see him, which should be in about a billion years."

All resistance melted beneath his sister's scornful stare. Bennett picked up the cookie bag and followed Addie into the house. The front door shut behind them on its own, and the numerous locks *clunked* into place.

"I have a bad feeling about this," Bennett whispered.

"Have you ever had a good feeling?"

They tried to follow their host's instructions, but it was too dark to even see a staircase.

"Some light would help," Addie yelled.

A pained sigh could be heard. "Is there no end to my misery?"

Two rows of recessed lighting in the ceiling came alive, albeit at reduced power, painting the surroundings in a fuzzy haze. The entranceway was obviously extravagant, with a grand staircase, carved wood paneling, marble flooring, and a crystal chandelier, but when Addie and Bennett began ascending to the second floor, they found the staircase railing coated in dust.

Addie wiped her hand on her skirt. "When was the last time you cleaned this place?"

"Turn right at the top of the stairs," the mysterious voice said, "and then it's the third door on the left."

They did as they were told, but Addie stopped when she spotted an elevator along the far wall. "There's an elevator? We've been walking all day, why'd you make us take the stairs?"

"You're young, you'll get over it. But hurry. I'm already tiring of your presence."

Addie whispered to Bennett, "This guy seems like a real jerk."

"I heard that," the voice said.

"How?"

"Third door on the—"

"Yeah, yeah, we know."

The designated door was slightly ajar, and Addie carefully eased it open. The room had only a dresser, a nightstand with a lamp, and a twin bed, making it fairly standard sleeping quarters. However, there was one surprising detail: The occupant of the aforementioned bed was a chimpanzee.

The chimp in question was tucked in under the covers and wearing pajamas, appearing as though he had just woken up from a nap. He tapped the screen of a digital tablet a few times and then placed it on the bed beside him.

"Took you long enough," he said. "Let's see those cookies."

CHAPTER FIVE

"You're a monkey!" Addie said.

"I'm not a monkey. I'm a chimpanzee."

"But you're talking." Addie turned to Bennett. "Are you seeing this?"

Her brother adjusted his glasses. "It's a talking monkey all right."

The chimp raised a finger in protest. "Eh…."

"Sorry," Bennett said. "Chimpanzee."

"But monkeys don't talk," Addie said.

"Chimpanzee," the chimp said. "I hate to belabor the point, but it really is quite insulting. Is she always this rude?"

"Pretty much," Bennett said.

Addie stared at her brother in disbelief. "You're talking to a monkey. Why are you acting like this is normal?"

"I've never met a monk—," Bennett caught himself, "—chimpanzee. Maybe they can talk."

"Ordinary chimpanzees cannot," the chimp said. "But I am far from ordinary. Now, I do believe there was some mention of banana cream cookies."

"This is nuts," Addie said. "I thought a great detective lived here."

"Guilty as charged. Sebastian Winthrop at your service. However, if I may correct you yet again, I am the great *retired* detective. Don't really do the detective thing anymore."

"But you're a monkey. Monkeys can't be detectives."

The great Sebastian Winthrop yawned and stretched, his hairy wrists extending beyond the cuffs of his wine-colored pajama top. "Once again, I'm not a monkey. I'm a chimpanzee."

"What's the difference?"

Sebastian laughed. "Now who's the monkey?"

"They're the same thing."

"Actually," Bennett said, "monkeys and chimpanzees are both primates, but chimpanzees belong to the great apes with gorillas, orangutans, and humans."

"Correct," Sebastian said. "But let's not forget our brothers the bonobos. What's your name, young man?"

"Bennett. And this is my sister Addie."

"You clearly got all the smarts in the family, Bennett, so please tell your ignorant little sister here the other significant differences between monkeys and chimpanzees."

"Monkeys have tails. Chimpanzees don't."

"And?" Sebastian said.

Bennett thought for a moment. "Chimpanzees have bigger brains and are smarter than monkeys."

"There it is." Sebastian pointed to himself. "Chimpanzee." He pointed to Addie. "Monkey. Now, let's have a go at those cookies."

Addie scrunched her face in anger and tossed a box of cookies on the bed. "They're five bucks."

"Seems a bit exorbitant." Sebastian studied the bright yellow box, the front of which featured three Pioneer Scouts happily strolling a sun-drenched meadow. "You know these girls?"

"No."

"Keep it that way. They've got shifty eyes." He read the nutritional information and ingredients. "Not exactly healthy, are they? You should be ashamed of yourself. Pushing diabetes and heart disease door to door on an unsuspecting populace. How much are they paying you?"

"We don't get paid."

"What? You're letting these capitalist pigs profit off your sweat and toil, and you don't even get a cut? What a sap."

"We get a badge."

"Yippee, a badge. That'll keep the lights on." He tore open the box and slid out a cellophane-wrapped sleeve of cookies.

"Hey, you just bought those, I hope you know."

"Depending on how they taste, you may be having that discussion with my attorney." Sebastian pulled free one of the white chocolate-covered cookies and gave it a sniff. "And you had nothing to do with producing these, correct?"

Addie shook her head.

"That's a relief." Sebastian turned the cookie slowly between his dexterous chimp fingers and inspected it for imperfections. He took his first taste, demonstrating the dainty nibble of a dignified gentleman. "Oh, will you look at that. We've got the chocolate on the outside, banana cream in the middle, and a cookie wafer at the bottom there. How clever." He sampled it again, taking a bigger bite this time. "Not too shabby." The remaining cookie disappeared. "Let me just try one or two more…." With a surprisingly energetic outburst, the chimp ripped apart the wrapper and gobbled the remaining cookies like a dirt-starved vacuum cleaner, shoving one handful after another into his overstuffed mouth.

After the mad flurry ended and his cookie-swollen cheeks thinned enough to allow speech, Sebastian wiped the crumbs from his mouth with the cuff of his satin pajama top and said, "The cookies are adequate. I will take one thousand boxes, please."

Addie, still somewhat stunned by what she had just witnessed, said, "We don't have a thousand boxes."

"How many do you have?"

Bennett rummaged through the contents of the shopping bag. "Two."

"What kind of an operation are you running here?"

"People don't usually buy banana cream," Addie said.

"That's because people are stupid. I'll take both boxes. What is that? Ten bucks?"

"Fifteen."

"I thought you said they were five dollars apiece?"

"You ate a box already."

"That wasn't a free sample? You really are the worst. Fine. Fifteen dollars." Sebastian accepted the cookie boxes from Bennett and placed them on the bed next to him. He lifted a chunky tri-fold wallet, its tattered brown leather held together with dull gray duct tape, from the cluttered nightstand.

"You need a new wallet," Addie said.

"You need to mind your own business." Sebastian opened the wallet. "Hmm, I seem to be a bit low on cash at the moment. Do you accept Ooh-Ooh-Ah-Ah coin?"

Addie and Bennett exchanged a confused look.

"Don't tell me you've never heard of Ooh-Ooh-Ah-Ah coin. It's the hottest cryptocurrency on the market. I created it myself. And I would be willing to give you one Ooh-Ooh-Ah-Ah coin in exchange for the cookies. By this time next year, that same Ooh-Ooh-Ah-Ah coin could be worth thousands of dollars."

"You're going to give us thousands of dollars for three boxes of cookies?"

"No, I will give you one Ooh-Ooh-Ah-Ah coin for the cookies. And that coin could one day be worth thousands of dollars."

"How much is it worth now?"

"Think of the earning potential."

"But how much is it worth today?"

"That's not the point. You need to consider the—"

Addie swiped the cookie boxes from the bed. "No cash, no cookies. But…we could make a trade. Our dad got arrested, and we need a detective to prove he's innocent. How about we give you the cookies, and you take our dad's case?"

"I assure you, my services cost more than three measly boxes of cookies. And what is it that your father did? Run a redlight? Cheat on his taxes?"

"He murdered a guy."

"Allegedly," Bennett added.

"Our dad is a professional wrestler. Well, he's a mechanic, but he wrestles on the weekends for the local promotion, Keystone Championship Wrestling. And Mitch Mayhem, the guy who got croaked, buried our dad in his last match, even though Mitch was a babyface champ and our dad had been built up as a monster heel."

"She means that Mitch was the good guy and our dad was the villain," Bennett said. "And Mitch beat our dad easily and made him look bad."

"No need to explain," Sebastian said. "I am highly knowledgeable about professional wrestling, like I am most everything. But I had no idea there was a local indie promotion. I don't get out much."

Addie said, "So, if you like wrestling, that means you know it's fake, right?"

"Fake? Professional wrestling isn't fake. Are the Greek tragedies fake? Is *Romeo and Juliet* fake? Pro wrestling is the ultimate drama. Tales of betrayal, triumph, and tragedy designed to manipulate emotions through physicality. Good versus evil. The lovable underdog rising up to overcome impossible odds. The dastardly heel receiving rightful justice for his unscrupulous deeds. Professional wrestling is the ideal, what society should strive to be. I assure you, professional wrestling is far from fake. Lord knows it's realer than whatever silly shows you watch about ponies and princesses."

"I don't watch TV shows about ponies and princesses." Bennett appeared ready to voice protest until the point of Addie's elbow kept him quiet. "But you don't have to tell us. We love wrestling. Just wanted to make sure you've been smartened up. Last thing we need is some stupid mark trying to solve the case."

"Who said I was going to do anything?"

"But you have to. Our dad is innocent."

"If he's so innocent, why did they arrest him?"

Bennett said, "There's some evidence that makes it look like he could have possibly done it. Sort of."

"What evidence?"

"I don't know," Addie said, dismissing the question with a careless flick of her hand. "Something dumb like him being at the scene of the crime and having his fingerprints on the murder weapon. They've got nothin', I tell ya, and they know it."

"That actually sounds like something. But I told you, my detective days are over. Solid gone."

"So, you're a quitter?"

"I wouldn't say I'm a quitter necessarily."

"But you quit."

"I'm just tired. Tired of the lies. Tired of the nonsense. Tired of pretending I'm stupid so everyone else feels better about the world they live in."

"Oh, so you're a tired quitter? Got it."

"I'm not a—"

"But we need your help. We know Daddy didn't do it. We've got a list of suspects and their reasons for killing Mitch. Bennett, show him the notebook."

Bennett slipped off his backpack and pulled from its unzipped pouch a school composition book. "We broke down the suspects by—"

"Save it, kid. There's nothing I can do."

"Sure, there is," Addie said. "No one is going to listen to us. We need a real detective to help find clues and interview people and—"

"I told you. I'm not a detective anymore. The world is a cesspool of greed and corruption. Politicians are puppets. The media spew nonstop propaganda. Everyone is so busy trying to prove what good people they are, they pass judgement and vilify anyone who dares question authority. Corporate tyranny runs amok. Commercialism rules the day. And the global elite have crushed all resistance beneath the jackboot of willful ignorance. Truth died long ago. What can one chimpanzee do to stem the tide? I ran my race. I fought my fight. And I lost. Now, I just want to be left alone."

"Okay, I don't know what any of that means," Addie said. "And honestly, you sound nuts—"

"Exactly my point."

"But you're our best chance to prove that our dad is innocent. You have to help."

"I don't have to do anything."

"You can't just—"

"Sure I can. What don't you understand? I can't help you. The well has run dry. Please show yourselves out so I can go back to sleep and forget this unfortunate encounter ever happened."

Addie closed her eyes, balled her hands into fists, and screamed, "But I didn't do it!"

The anguished wail caused Bennett to recoil and the supposed great detective to duck beneath the covers for protection. Sebastian peeked out from beneath the blankets and saw a solitary tear meandering down Addie's cheek. "What did you say?"

"You have to help us because I know he didn't do it."

"That's not what you said." Sebastian returned to his full sitting position. "You said, 'But *I* didn't do it.'"

Addie, unable to look anywhere but the floor, wiped away the tear. "No, I didn't."

"Yeah, you did," Bennett said. "You don't think you're responsible for this, do you?"

"If I hadn't made fun of Daddy for not standing up to Mitch, he never would have gotten so angry and…you know." Her head somehow managed to sink even lower. "It's all my fault. Daddy's going to prison. Mommy and him will get divorced. Our stepdad will probably be some goof named Kyle who won't even let us watch wrestling, and I'll have to take ballet and piano lessons and…I ruined everything."

"Don't cry, Addie," Bennett said, hugging his sister. "If Sebastian won't help us, we'll keep trying until we find someone who will. We'll figure something out."

Addie buried her face in her brother's boney chest and continued weeping, her puny frame heaving with each fitful sob.

Sebastian stared at the pitiful pair through moist eyes. He bit his lower lip and breathed deep through his nose, attempting to steel his nerves and resist the urge to make what he knew would be a regrettable decision. But the sight of the sad siblings was too much. "I'll help you."

Addie's wailing stopped. She glanced up at Sebastian from her brother's comforting embrace. "Really?"

"I have some connections at City Hall." Sebastian pawed at his right eye as if clearing it of anything but a tear. "We'll go talk to your father. And if I think he's telling the truth, I'll take the case. But this isn't charity. And I don't work cheap."

"But we don't have any money," Bennett said, his sister still clinging to him.

"Then I guess my fee will be…three boxes of banana cream cookies."

Addie disengaged from Bennett and wiped the remaining tears from her face. "You mean it?"

Sebastian offered his hand. "My word is my bond."

Addie looked to Bennett, who gave her a slight nod of approval. She inched forward, and after a brief moment of trepidation, she clasped the chimp's hand. The contract sealed, she hopped back and pointed at Sebastian, her once tear-soaked eyes laughing with delight. "Ha! I knew you were a mark."

"You worked me?"

"Darn right I did. Now get your little monkey pants on and let's go. We've got a murder to solve!"

CHAPTER SIX

The hallway outside Sebastian Winthrop's bedroom was extraordinary—Brazilian cherry hardwood flooring, ivory raised-panel wainscotting, muted yellow walls, and a series of framed portraits lining each side of the lengthy corridor. Yes, a truly magnificent hallway. But a terrible waiting room.

"How long does it take a monkey to get dressed?" Addie said, pacing. "This is ridiculous."

Bennett, who was sitting cross-legged on the floor reading an arithmetic textbook, ignored his sister's impatience, a skill he had cultivated through years of practice.

Addie hammered on the bedroom door with her fist. "Hey, your highness. We're waiting out here."

"One moment please," Sebastian called from behind the door. "Almost ready."

Addie resumed her petulant pacing. "*One moment* he says. Daddy's rotting in prison, and he's in there fixing his hair."

"You should really be nicer to him," Bennett said. "He's the only one who's going to help us."

"I'm starting to think this whole idea of yours was a big mistake."

"This wasn't my—"

"What can he really do, anyway? We need a real detective. If no one will listen to us, why would they listen to a talking monkey?"

"Actually, I think a lot of people would want to listen to a talking monkey."

Addie studied one of the many portraits decorating the walls. This particular one depicted a middle-aged gentleman with short gray hair dressed in a black turtleneck and beige sport coat. "And who are all these weirdos? Would you want paintings of these guys in our house? I'm telling ya, this monkey ain't right. I have a half a mind to—"

The bedroom door opened. "That's half a mind more than I thought you had," Sebastian said, stepping into the hall. His lengthy preparation produced a casual aristocratic ensemble of a plum silk smoking jacket with black cuffs, lapels, and belt over a white shirt, gray gabardine slacks, and black wingtip Oxford shoes. A royal blue ascot tied it all together.

"You look stupid," Addie said.

"This coming from a girl dressed like a fascist."

"I don't know what that means."

"Of course you don't. But I assure you, this smoking jacket is not stupid."

"You shouldn't smoke, Monkey. It's bad for you."

"I don't smoke. I'm fashionable." Sebastian brushed past Addie and headed down the hall. "Chop, chop. No time to waste."

Bennett and Addie gathered their backpacks and cookie-filled shopping bag and hurried to catch up to the departing chimp.

"You kept us out here forever," Addie said. "And who are all these guys in the paintings?"

"This is my Hall of Heroes," Sebastian said. "They are the greatest detectives known to man or chimp. Lieutenant Columbo. Thomas Banacek. Sam McCloud. Stewart McMillan. Quincy. The fact you don't recognize any of them is a scathing indictment of the American educational system."

Addie pointed at a portrait of a smiling old man with plump rosy cheeks, a large nose, and an even bigger white mustache. "He doesn't look like a detective."

"That's because he wasn't."

"Then who is he?"

Sebastian stopped at the elevator doors. "He's my father."

"How can he be your father? He's a dude, and you're a monkey."

"Not my biological father, you twit. He's the man who raised me."

"Does he live here too?"

Sebastian pushed the elevator button. "He's dead."

"What about him?" Bennett said. He indicated a portrait of a black cat, whose erect posture and knowing eyes denoted a sense of regal nobility. "Was he a detective?"

"No, he was my best friend." The elevator doors opened, and Sebastian stepped inside. "He's dead too."

Addie and Bennett shared a quick glance, unsure exactly what to say, and then joined Sebastian in the elevator. They silently watched him press a button marked F on a shiny gold panel.

"Gee, Monkey," Addie said. "Sounds like you've had it pretty rough."

"It's been years. At least I think it has. Who can tell, really? Down we go."

The elevator began its smooth, steady descent, the hum of its operation barely discernible through the Persian carpet and carved mahogany paneling.

"Where we going?"

"To the garage. I assume you didn't intend to conduct this investigation on foot."

"They let you drive a car?"

Sebastian gave her a dirty look.

"It wasn't meant to be mean. Just seems surprising that they'd give a license to a m—"

"Chimpanzee," Bennett said, in an attempt to calm the situation.

The elevator eased to a halt, and when the doors slid open, banks of overhead fluorescent lights crackled to life, revealing a cavernous garage that could have doubled as an automobile showroom. A center lane, so designated by thin white lines running the length of the dark green epoxy flooring, divided two columns of glistening vehicles. The reflective steel plating on the walls made the room seem even more spacious, and the assorted storage lockers, workbenches, and tool chests arranged along the perimeter seemed miles away.

"Wow, you really are rich," Addie said. "If this is where you keep all your cars, what's on those other floors we passed on the way down?"

"Let's hope we don't know each other long enough for you to find out." Sebastian ambled among his waiting vehicles like a sergeant inspecting his troops. "What should it be today?"

Addie ran up to a candy-apple red muscle car with a distinctive white stripe that jutted down from the roof to the rear wheels and then thinned to a point at the front bumper. "Let's take this one."

"That is a 1975 Ford Gran Torino, identical to the one owned by Detective David Starsky of the crime-fighting duo Starsky and Hutch. But we can't take it out today."

"Why not?"

"I could lie to you and say it's out of gas or is having transmission problems or the like, but frankly…I don't know where you've been, and I really don't want you in it."

Bennett, still lugging the bag of cookies and his oversized backpack, set his sights on a gold Pontiac Firebird. "This one's cool."

"Would Jim Rockford drive anything that wasn't?"

"Who's Joe Rockton?" Addie said.

"Jim Rockford. The incomparable James Garner played him on *The Rockford Files*. Do you children have no culture at all? Looks like it's up to me to correct the failures of your parents, teachers, and society at large." Sebastian pointed out the significance of each car in his extensive collection, which numbered more than two dozen and included Lieutenant Columbo's Peugeot, Kojak's Buick Century, and Thomas Magnum's Ferrari 308 GTS. By the time he got to Frank

Cannon's metallic blue Lincoln Continental, his audience's meager attention span had run out.

"Can we just go already?" Addie whined. "You're killing me here, Monkey."

"Forgive me. I assumed you would like to learn something and enhance your peanut-sized brain. My mistake. But if you're in such a hurry, we'll just take Ol' Blue."

Sebastian turned in a huff and headed toward the end of the left column of cars. Addie and Bennett watched him get into a light blue, two-door compact car that couldn't possibly have starred in any old TV shows.

"What the heck is this?" Addie said, doing little to hide her disgust.

"*This* is a 1989 Pontiac LeMans. The Cadillac of hatchbacks." Sebastian swung into the driver's seat and reached over to unlock the passenger side. "It has character."

Bennett opened the door for his sister, and Addie climbed into the back seat. She was the perfect size to squeeze into the cramped quarters. "But you have all those other great cars," she said. "Why do you drive this hunk of junk?"

"This was my father's car. First, you make fun of the wallet he gave me, and now you're ridiculing his car? What a creep. And for a supposed *hunk of junk*, it still turns plenty of heads."

"Yeah, they're all wondering who let a monkey drive a shoebox."

Bennett managed to get the cookie bag into the back with Addie and then situated his backpack on the floor between his feet. When he finally got the door shut and his seatbelt fastened, he turned to Sebastian and said, "I like it."

"Of course you do," Sebastian said. "Because you're smart, unlike a certain other individual who shall remain nameless. What was that book I saw you reading earlier?"

"An algebra textbook."

"Did you lose a bet?"

"No," Addie said, "he likes to do math during the summer because he's a dorkus malorkus."

Bennett shifted uncomfortably in his seat. "I just want to be ready for eighth-grade math."

"What grade are you in now?"

"I'm going into fourth," Addie said, not letting her brother answer. "He's going into sixth. Yet he's already worried about eighth grade. Can you believe it? What a maroon."

"That's very impressive, Bennett," Sebastian said. "Shows tremendous initiative. It's that kind of dedication and hard work that makes a great detective."

"Hey, I work plenty hard too," Addie said. "I was third in my class last year."

"I'm sure all the other chihuahuas at the kennel club were green with envy."

Addie delivered a forearm shiver to the back of Bennett's seat to stifle his laughing. "Shut up and drive, Monkey."

The alleged Cadillac of hatchbacks wheezed its way out of the main garage and down a long tunnel toward an apparent dead end. However, when Ol' Blue approached, the steel barrier disappeared into the ceiling with a sudden *whoosh*, and then a second obstruction slid into the right wall before a third vanished into the ground, enabling the car to emerge from the dimly lit underworld into the afternoon sun. Addie and Bennett spun in their seats to see a section of the prodigious hill they had climbed earlier to reach Sebastian's house flip shut, the grassy landscape and shrubbery betraying no hint of the secret entrance.

"How'd you do that?" Bennett said.

Sebastian steered the car off the private auxiliary road and turned toward downtown. "The same way one does anything. Money."

"Since when do detectives make so much money?" Addie said.

"Normal detectives don't."

Addie scootched forward and stretched for the radio. "Let's listen to some music."

Sebastian slapped her hand away. "The radio doesn't work."

"Then why don't you get it fixed, Moneybags."

"Nostalgia. Bennett, open the glovebox, please. There should be a tape recorder inside loaded with my favorite song."

Bennett pulled the handle to open the glovebox, and it came off in his hand.

"Don't worry," Sebastian said. "Happens all the time. Just sort of jam it back in there and give it a good whack."

Bennett did as he was told, and after two failed attempts, the glovebox fell open. Sure enough, there was an ancient tape recorder inside. He pushed *Play*.

They heard the loud, shrill sounds of a calliope, followed by a playful arrangement of woodwinds and short bursts of tuba. Sebastian immediately started bopping his head to the kooky arrangement.

"You gotta be joking me," Addie said. "What is this nonsense?"

"*Baby Elephant Walk* by Henry Mancini."

Addie reached for the *Stop* button. "Turn it off."

"No," Bennett said, pulling the tape recorder to safety. He and Sebastian shared a smile.

Addie covered her ears and slumped into the back seat. "You're both weirdos."

The remaining drive to City Hall was spent with *Baby Elephant Walk* blaring and Sebastian and Bennett bouncing to the peppy tune.

"How long is this stupid song?" Addie asked, still plugging her ears.

"Only song on the tape," Sebastian said. "Sixty minutes both sides. Yet somehow, it never seems long enough."

CHAPTER SEVEN

The Hadleyburg Police Department operated out of City Hall, a rectangular orange-brick building with all the allure of a rotten kumquat. Located on Main Street in the heart of town, the department was home to twenty-seven police officers and seventeen civilian support staff, all of whom were charged with protecting and serving Hadleyburg's roughly 15,000 residents. On this day, three of those residents—consisting of two children and one chimp—ascended the front steps on a mission for justice…or at least some additional banana cream cookies.

Sebastian paused at the entrance to provide final instructions to his two employers. "Remember, follow my lead. And under no circumstances should you—what are you doing?"

Addie was rattling her skull like an empty piggy back. "Can't get that song out of my head."

"At least there's something in there. Now straighten up and try to look presentable. These people would like to be my peers."

Sebastian opened the door and ushered Addie and Bennett into a sterile closet that served as a poor excuse for a foyer. Straight ahead was a steel door with a thin vertical window filled with meshed security glass. To the right was a receptionist area protected by bulletproof glass and a sign that read PAY PARKING TICKETS HERE. A young woman, whose lack of the standard uniform indicated a civilian, appeared at the window. "Can I help—" But the offer of assistance was cut short when she saw a smiling Sebastian between Addie and Bennett. "I'm sorry, but I don't think you can bring your monkey in here."

Confused, Sebastian looked around before chuckling. "Oh, I see your mistake." He placed his hand on Addie's shoulder. "This is my niece, not a monkey. But could you please tell Detective Raymond Carter that Sebastian Winthrop is here to see him."

"I'm sorry…you want…wait, what?"

"Detective Raymond Carter. He's expecting us."

Without taking her eyes from Sebastian, the young woman reached for the desk phone and punched in Detective Carter's extension. "There's a Sebastian Winthrop to see you." Upon receiving approval, she pressed a button that unlatched the security door. "Go right in."

Sebastian gave a slight salute. "Thank you, miss. You're a credit to the department."

They were barely through the door when a man in an out-of-style blue suit whirled around the corner. His hairline had receded on top, leaving a peninsula of hair amidst a sea of high forehead, and he moved with the size and lumbering gait of a former football player who had suffered one too many knee injuries. "You're late."

"Couldn't be helped," Sebastian said, falling in line at the man's hip and continuing a deliberate trajectory down the hall. "Was righting a terrible wrong."

The man nodded to Addie and Bennett, who were trailing behind. "Who are they?"

"Two ruffians who didn't know who Columbo was. I learned them but good. Is he in the holding cells?"

"Yeah, but we have to hustle. The chief could be back any minute."

Addie looked up at Detective Carter. "You know you're talking to a monkey, right?"

"Don't mind her," Sebastian said. "She was dropped on her head as a baby. Repeatedly."

Detective Carter guided them down two flights of stairs to the basement, where they passed through another steel security door, to which Carter had a key, before entering a long narrow room. A lone officer sat behind a desk reading a newspaper, his light blue uniform shirt conjuring images of cotton candy against the pale pink concrete-block walls.

"Got some visitors for Pajakowski," Detective Carter said. "Will just be a minute."

The officer looked up from his sports section and saw Sebastian grinning back at him.

"Good to see you again, Officer Harlow."

The officer seemed far less excited to see Sebastian. "Uh, should he be here?"

Detective Carter motioned for Sebastian, Addie, and Bennett to go on ahead and hung back to talk to his colleague. "Listen, Ernie. Let's just keep this little visit between us."

"If the chief finds out I let you—"

"You weren't even here." Detective Carter took out his wallet and dropped five dollars on the desk. "You were upstairs getting the prisoner something to eat."

Officer Harlow looked at the fancy chimp leading two children into the holding area and then considered the money on the desk. "I don't know, Ray. I think the prisoner is hungrier than that."

Another five hit the desk.

"He hasn't eaten all day."

Detective Carter fanned the remaining cash in his wallet. "I only have three ones."

Officer Harlow pocketed the bills. "You'll owe me." He gathered the rest of the money and was off like a shot.

Addie and Bennett's father had heard the commotion and came to the front of his cell to see what was going on. Addie raced ahead of Sebastian and Bennett to greet him. "Daddy!"

"Addie Bug!" The hulking professional wrestler dropped down on one knee and tried to hug his daughter through the bars. Bennett was quick to join them. "Benny!"

"We miss you, Daddy," Addie said. "But don't worry, we're gonna get you out of here."

"We hired a detective," Bennett said.

"What are you talking about? And where's Mom?" He stood up and pressed himself against the unforgiving iron bars to get a better view. But instead of his wife, he saw something that his brain couldn't quite comprehend.

"Sebastian Winthrop. I am the aforementioned detective."

Pajakowski, bewilderment painted on his slack-jawed face, cautiously reached through the cell bars and shook the chimp's hand. "You're a talking monkey."

Addie shoved her brother. "Told you."

"I certainly see where Addie gets her social graces." Sebastian took a handkerchief from his pocket and wiped his hand. "But your children have convinced me to take an interest in your case. I am here to determine whether the cause is worthy."

Detective Carter said, "I can vouch for Sebastian's skills as a detective. He may be a chimpanzee, but his credentials are legit, and he's already helped me on a couple of particularly challenging cases since he's been in town."

Addie scowled at Sebastian. "I thought you said you're retired?"

"Retired, not dead. I get bored."

"I've already told Sebastian that I think you're innocent," Detective Carter said, "but the chief has my hands tied. According to him, the case is closed. Bringing in Sebastian might be our best bet."

Pajakowski scratched his enormous head. He looked like a caged gorilla perplexed by the intricacies of a tire swing. "I guess. I mean, you've shot straight with me, Detective Carter. And I need all the help I can get." He reached through the bars once more. "Thank you, Mr. Monkey Man. I will be honored to have you work my case."

Sebastian reluctantly accepted a second handshake. "Yes, well, whether I take the case must still be determined. How was Mr. Pajakowski connected to the murder so quickly?"

"A neighbor spotted a man who matched his description arriving at the property shortly after eleven p.m. on the night in question," Detective Carter said. "The same neighbor discovered the body the following morning when she noticed that the front door of

Mitch's house was open while walking her dog." He lifted a notepad from his suitcoat pocket and quickly flipped to the desired page. "The woman, a Mrs. Agnes Floozle, stated that the man she saw was 'Very large and wearing a black wrestling outfit like that Andre the Giant fella.' I spoke with a Mr. Tony Katsaros, the promoter of Keystone Championship Wrestling, and he informed me that Mr. Pajakowski fit the description."

"You were at the scene?" Sebastian said to Pajakowski, still discretely wiping off the remnants of their most recent handshake on his trouser leg.

"Yeah, like I told Detective Carter, I went there to have it out with Mitch about our match. He made me look pretty bad, and he was ruining the locker room, so I wanted to hash things out. And that's what we did. It wasn't anything bad. No arguing. No yelling. He actually apologized, and the whole thing went way better than I expected. Can't tell you how relieved I was. I swear, he was alive when I left."

"How did your fingerprints end up on the murder weapon?"

Detective Carter indicated Addie and Bennett with a subtle nod. "Should we be talking about this in front of—"

"Oh, puh-lease," Addie said. She poked Detective Carter in the belly. "We know more about this case than you do, buddy. Listen up, Monkey. Mitch Mayhem had his brains smashed in with one of his Squared Circle awards. Daddy probably touched it when he was there talking to Mitch. Right, Daddy?"

"That's true. We were discussing his career, and I probably touched a few of the awards."

"Then the real murderer comes along and happens to grab the same award." Addie demonstrated a sadistic two-handed swing. "BLAM-O! Scrambled eggs."

Detective Carter buttoned his sport coat to protect against further belly poking. "That's more or less what happened. The victim was struck in the back of the head with one of his own wrestling trophies, and the blow was so strong that it snapped off the trophy's marble base. The killer took the rest of the weapon with him. And the only clear prints belonged to Mr. Pajakowski."

"What's the Squared Circle?" Sebastian asked.

"It's this stupid online newsletter written by some old geezer," Addie said.

"Actually," her father said, "it's a respected news source."

Addie laughed. "For rumors and nonsense."

"It's written by Steve Thacker, a veteran journalist."

"Journalist?" She rolled her eyes like Yahtzee dice. "More like the biggest mark who ever lived."

"Hey, winning one of his awards is a big honor."

"Yeah, if you're an internet nerd with no friends."

"Regardless," Sebastian said, hoping to put an end to the father–daughter dance, "who else could have wanted Mitch dead?"

Addie ignored that the question was directed to her father. "Lots of people. And we tried to tell you earlier, but you wouldn't listen. Open up those monkey ears and pay attention this time. Bennett, tell him."

Bennett, who had comfortably melted into the background during the entire discussion, flushed at suddenly being pulled upon center stage.

"Go ahead, Benny," his dad said. "You can do it."

Emboldened by his father's support, Bennett adjusted his glasses and took a deep breath. "We narrowed it down to four main suspects. First is Vince Manero. Mitch took his spot and pushed him down the card. Manero is also getting older, and he probably wasn't going to get a shot at the title again as long as Mitch was around."

"I only got my program with Mitch because he refused to give Manero a title shot."

Detective Carter added, "And the championship belt is missing. It's presumed that whoever murdered Mitch stole the belt."

"Manero's got this stupid rock star gimmick," Addie said. "He's so lame."

"C'mon, Addie," her father said. "It's not *that* bad."

Addie cupped her hands around her mouth like a megaphone and screamed, "Lame!"

"You would be the authority," Sebastian said. "Who's next, Bennett?"

"Mad Mike Dean. He's a hardcore, death-match wrestler."

"Dean was Mitch's tag partner a long time ago," their father said. "But their relationship soured over the years."

"For a supposed tough guy, he throws the phoniest punches I've ever seen," Addie said. She demonstrated the questionable striking technique, flailing her arms like wet noodles.

"Third would be Lenny Lambda," Bennett said. "Most everybody thinks he's the best wrestler in the company."

"Not me." Addie got up on her tiptoes and imitated the movements of what appeared to be a deranged muskrat. "He prances around the ring and is super dramatic. Spirit fingers and everything. Does a bunch of flashy flips without selling any moves. The guy's a clown."

Sebastian said, "Is there anyone you like?"

"Yeah, real professional wrestlers, like Daddy. Not trampoline cowboys and theater kids playing make-believe."

"But why would this Lambda guy want Mitch dead?"

"After he beat me, Mitch cut a promo in the ring that made fun of Lambda and his friends, the Hickson Brothers. They heard about it and started a fight with him in the dressing room."

"We were there," Addie said. "It was awesome."

"But are a few insults enough to murder someone?"

Addie shook a fist at the chimp. "Keep making fun of me, and you're gonna find out."

"It was more than a few insults. There had been a lot of heat between Mitch and Lambda for months."

"Over what?"

"I guess you could say creative differences."

"Yeah," Addie said, "Mitch, while a big jerk, knew good wrestling. He didn't like Lambda's stupid flippy-dippy stuff either."

"There was a power struggle behind the scenes. Mitch and Lambda both had Tony's ear, and they had different views of what they wanted the promotion to be."

"Who's Tony?" Sebastian asked.

"Tony Katsaros. He owns the promotion."

"His rich *dad* owns the promotion," Addie corrected. "Tiny Tony just gets to play with it. You should see this guy, Monkey. He dresses worse than you."

"He's also our fourth suspect," Bennett said. "He was pretty mad at Mitch."

"Tony was working on a TV deal with one of the local stations," their father said. "He had some executives in attendance when Mitch cut his promo and the backstage fight broke out, so he was pretty hot. May have ruined the deal."

Sebastian counted the suspects on his fingers. "We have Manero the aging rock star, Dean the hardcore wrestler, Lambda the flippy guy, and Tony the promoter."

"What do you think, Sebastian?" Detective Carter said.

"I just have one question for Mr. Pajakowski." Sebastian stood straight with his hands behind his back and addressed the prisoner. "Did you do it?"

Pajakowski looked at his children, who stared back at him with imploring eyes, before answering. "No, no, of course not. I'm innocent."

Sebastian walked up to the cell bars and motioned for Pajakowski to come closer. The weekend wrestler seemed uncomfortable with the request, but he once again dropped to one knee and met the chimp's unflinching scrutiny. Now nose to nose, Sebastian squinted his potential client into focus, his intense concentration pressing his lips into a hard line. "Did you do it?"

Pajakowski swallowed hard. "No."

Sebastian straightened the hem of his smoking jacket and smoothed any unbecoming creases. He then turned and stepped toward Detective Carter. "I believe that—" Sebastian spun and pointed at Pajakowski. "Did you do it?"

Pajakowski staggered backward. "No. Honest, I swear."

"Welp, guess he didn't do it. I'll take the case."

Addie and Bennett's celebratory fist pumps were rudely interrupted when a distinctly Canadian voice bellowed, "Where is he, eh? Where's that monkey?"

Detective Carter's shoulders sagged. "Oh no."

Into the room rolled an angry bowling ball with legs. The man hitched up his belt with each heavy-footed stomp of his mukluk boots, his gray uniform pants clearly losing an ongoing battle with his protruding belly. His fleshy cheeks glowed crimson from either fury or exertion, and atop his pumpkin-sized head sat a red knit tuque with a white pom pom—a clear uniform violation for anyone not sledding in Saskatchewan.

"There's the mangy hoser," the man said, his pencil-thin red mustache an affront to facial hair. "Thought I smelled somethin' prissy."

Sebastian sniffed his smoking jacket. "That's actually lavender and vanilla, my own special blend. Perhaps I'll give you a bottle. You can add a few drops to your sty."

"Very funny, monkey. A real laugh riot you are, eh. We'll see how funny it is when I make a rug from your hide. And who are these kids?"

"They're my employers," Sebastian said. "Addie and Bennett Pajakowski, I would like you to meet Dominique Bouchard, the Chief of Police. Born in Canada, he was raised in Western Pennsylvania and has since made it his home away from the buffet table. But he never lets anyone forget that he was, indeed, born in Canada. That's Chief Bouchard, Canadian through and through. Cut him and he'd bleed maple syrup. How long did you live there, eighteen months?"

"Some of us are proud of where we come from and don't try to pretend we're something we're not. All the fancy smoking jackets in the world can't hide the fact that you're a stupid little monkey. But did you say their names are Pajakowski?" Chief Bouchard eyed his prisoner. "They belong to you?"

"Yes, sir."

"Carter, I don't recall approving any family visits. And I know I told you I never wanted to see that monkey in my police department ever again."

"I'm sorry, Chief, but Pajakowski's children have hired Sebastian to investigate his case, and I didn't want to—"

"Case?" Chief Bouchard said. "What case? That man right there is a murderer, eh, and I proved it. I don't need no big-city monkey comin' in here and tellin' me how to do my job."

Addie stepped forward with clenched fists. "Our dad's innocent."

Chief Bouchard stooped as far as his belly allowed to address Addie directly. "Your father is guilty, and he's going away to prison for a very, very long time. I'll see to that. And there's nothing you or some highfalutin monkey can do about it."

Chief Bouchard turned his back to her, and Addie attempted to fire a right cross into his posterior, but Bennett caught her arm and prevented another family member from ending up behind bars.

"Now, if you'll excuse me," Chief Bouchard said, waddling his way from the room, "I believe it's time for my afternoon poutine. Carter, if those individuals—especially that flea-bitten keener—are not off the premises by the time I'm done, it'll be your badge."

Chief Bouchard departed, whistling *Oh, Canada* as he went. Sebastian was the first to speak, turning to Addie and saying, "Wow, he really hates you."

"Okay, everybody," Detective Carter said, "now's the time to say your goodbyes."

Addie and Bennett hugged their father, caring little for the iron bars between them. They shared heartfelt expressions of love and promised to stick together no matter what. Their father kissed each of them goodbye and then asked, "Hey, does Mommy miss me?"

Addie and Bennett looked at each other, silently deliberating a question that should have been easily answered.

"I think so," Addie said.

"You *think* so?"

"I mean, she hasn't said she doesn't."

Their father let his head fall forward against the bars in defeat. "It's okay. I can make it up to her. We'll get through this. Before you know it, I'll be home with you and Mommy. I'll be back fixing cars, wrestling on the weekends. It'll be like none of this ever happened. That reminds me, I need you to have Mommy call Mr. Winslow at the garage and update him on everything."

"I don't think we need to do that," Bennett said.

"Yeah, pretty sure they fired you as soon as this hit the news," Addie said.

Their father slowly bounced his head off the cell bars. "This is a nightmare. I'm gonna wake up any second now."

"Relax, Daddy. Aren't you forgetting something?" She smiled wide and pointed at Sebastian. "We hired a detective."

Sensing the Pajakowski family's hopeful stares, Sebastian halted his conversation with Detective Carter and offered a toothy grin in recognition.

Their father resumed headbutting the cell bars. "I'm doomed."

CHAPTER EIGHT

Returned to the secure confines of Ol' Blue, where he knew Chief Bouchard would be unable to overhear their discussions, Sebastian permitted Addie to voice the question that she had been dying to ask: "What's our first step, Monkey?"

Sebastian used his non-opposable thumbs to quickly type something into his cell phone. "We need to investigate the crime scene. Detective Carter was kind enough to give me the deceased's address, and if I know anything about Chief Bouchard and his men, they missed something."

"Why doesn't Chief Bouchard like you?" Bennett asked.

Addie, perched on the edge of the back seat, said, "I can think of a few reasons."

"I'll explain it like this," Sebastian said. "Everyone thinks they're smart. Then, when someone smarter comes along, they see that individual as a constant reminder of their own inferiority. I am just such a reminder for Chief Bouchard…and pretty much everyone, really. People often hate what they don't understand."

"I don't hate you," Bennett said.

"That's because you're highly intelligent and don't feel threatened by my uniqueness."

"You're not smarter than me," Addie said.

Sebastian finished studying the directions to the crime scene and placed his cell phone in the car's center console. "Never said I was."

"But you think you are."

"Never said that either."

"Because you're not."

"Okay."

Addie stared at Sebastian for several seconds—the chimp showing nothing but calm composure—before flopping into the back seat and crossing her arms. "Shut up and drive."

Sebastian placed the key in the ignition and froze.

"C'mon, Monkey," Addie said. "What are you waiting for?"

It took Bennett a moment before he realized the reason for the delay. Smiling, he plucked the tape recorder from the dashboard and pressed *Play*.

Addie screamed, "Noooooooooooo!"

* * *

Mitch Mayhem's house was an unassuming home located in a quaint residential neighborhood on the quiet part of town…which is a polite way of saying it was an ugly house in an even uglier neighborhood. Overgrown grass and unbridled dandelions indicated that the lawn had not been mowed for at least several weeks before the owner's untimely demise, and the green vinyl siding needed a good pressure washing. Sebastian pulled into the gravel driveway, which sloped down and around the house.

After her brother silenced the driving music, Addie asked, "Shouldn't we park down the street or something?"

"No need for stealth in this instance," Sebastian said. The trio exited the car and strode the stone walkway to the cement slab of a front porch. "The best way to go unnoticed is to act like you belong. If a nosy neighbor sees us skulking around the property, they might think we're up to no good. But if we park in the driveway and walk right up to the front door, they'll assume we're supposed to be here. Let that be your first of many lessons in detective work."

Sebastian tried to open the front door and found it locked.

"You actually thought it was going to be open?" Addie asked.

"No, I didn't actually think it was going to be open," Sebastian said in a mocking tone. "But one can't assume anything in this business. Trust but verify. Let that be lesson two. You know, I could charge good money for this stuff. You should really be taking no–"

"Hey, what are you kids doing over there?" shouted a raspy voice to their right.

The chimp detective and his two charges turned to discover an elderly woman hollering at them from the front porch of the neighboring house. She was partially shielded by her home's screen door, but her surliness was as unmistakable as her floral housecoat and curlers.

"Good afternoon," Sebastian said. "My colleagues and I were just—"

"The owner's dead. I don't like you snooping around his house."

Sebastian laughed. "I hardly think we're snooping. I mean, we walked right up to the front door like we belong here."

"You're snooping."

"Rest assured, madame, we're supposed to be here."

"Who says?"

"I don't see what business that is of yours."

"Go on, git. Before I call the cops."

Sebastian gestured nervously to Ol' Blue. "But we parked in the driveway."

"That does it." The old woman stepped out from behind the screen door and waved her cane as if thwarting imaginary buzzards. Addie and Bennett were so transfixed by the bizarre woman, they didn't notice Sebastian break into a desperate sprint for the car.

"Run!" yelled the retreating chimp over his shoulder.

Sebastian didn't wait for Addie and Bennett to get in before backing out of the driveway. Only when the car was on the street and pointed to freedom did he hesitate long enough for the two siblings to pile into the passenger seat. He took off before the car door shut.

Sebastian sped around the corner and traveled another block or two, during which time Addie and Bennett bounced around the front seat like tennis shoes in a dryer, before pulling next to a vacant lot and cutting the engine. He took a deep breath and released the steering wheel from his death grip.

"That was terrifying."

Addie righted herself and disentangled from her brother. "What the heck, Monkey? You were gonna leave us!"

"Not true." Sebastian turned his entire body in the driver's seat so that Addie could see the sincerity in his eyes. Then, in a calm, comforting tone, he said, "I would never leave Bennett."

"Thanks, Sebastian," Bennett said, using his T-shirt to remove a smudge from his glasses.

"No problem. But it's pretty obvious who the neighbor was who spotted your father at the scene of the crime. Perhaps this situation will require a bit of stealth after all. To the hatchback."

Sebastian took to the rear of the vehicle and introduced his crime-fighting companions to another of Ol' Blue's hidden features. "Very few people have ever had the honor of seeing what you're about to see. Prepare yourselves." He hesitated to give the children a chance to truly appreciate the significance of the moment, and then he inserted his key into the lock and popped the hatchback, the large rear window and attached tail section flipping open like a clam shell. Sebastian stepped aside so they could get a better view. "Nice, huh?"

The entire space was filled with a metal chest of drawers.

"I didn't know you liked to knit," Addie said.

Sebastian did a double-take. "What?"

"Our NiNi has something just like this to hold all her yarn and needles and stuff."

"What's a NiNi?"

"Our grandmother," Bennett said.

"And she's like a gazillion years old," Addie said. "Sure, it's a little weird that you have the same hobby as an old lady, but whatever."

"I can assure you that your *NiNi* —if that is her real name— has nothing like this. What you see before you is a meticulously organized detective toolbox that contains everything needed to conduct a proper investigation. No matter what problems arise, these drawers have the answer." He pointed to the top row of three thin compartments. "Up here, we have lockpicks, magnifying lenses, tweezers, mini-flashlights, and assorted hand tools." Next, he indicated six mid-sized drawers organized into two columns that filled the left half of the chest. "Here are high-tech tools, like listening devices, cameras, and audio recorders, as well as a few weapons in case things get rough."

Addie reached for one of the drawers. "I want to see the weapons."

Sebastian stepped in front of her. "No weapons. You're dangerous enough."

"C'mon, Monkey. Show us the guns."

"I don't have any guns."

"Yeah, the drawers are too small for guns," Bennett said.

"You're right," Addie said. "Probably knives. Or brass knuckles." She threw a few pretend punches. Then, her eyes lit up. "Or ninja stars!"

Bennett shared the excitement. "Really?"

"Forget the weapons," Sebastian said. "We're not gonna need them today. Our concern is—"

"Do you have ninja stars or don't you?" Addie said.

Sebastian pointed out a column of three drawers that constituted the right half of the chest. "This is what we'll be using today."

"Can't believe you have ninja stars and didn't even tell us."

"That old lady next door will be on the lookout. She will obviously recognize Ol' Blue, so we'll have to approach the house on foot from the rear. However, there's still a chance that she could spot us. But she will be looking for two children and an outrageously handsome detective." He pointed to the drawers on the right. "That's where these come in. These three drawers are filled with the best disguises money can buy. We will blend into the environment and become invisible to even the most trained observers."

Addie jumped up and down. "Ninja outfits!"

"Sort of."

* * *

Even if Agnes Floozle, the angry old woman with the cane, had been keeping a vigilant watch over the departed Mitch Mayhem's property rather than napping in her recliner to *Matlock* reruns, she never would have spotted the two children and the outrageously handsome detective she had chased away earlier. Such was the effectiveness of Sebastian's subterfuge. However, Agnes may have wondered why a pirate, cowboy, and construction worker were darting from bush to bush and ducking behind trees until finally making a mad dash across the truncated backyard.

The disguised detectives plastered themselves against the back wall of Mitch Mayhem's house and tried to catch their breaths.

"Did she see us?" Bennett asked, his cowboy hat sitting crooked on his head.

Sebastian leaned forward and flipped up his eyepatch to get a better look. "I think we're safe."

All three surveyed their surroundings. The rear of the home had two stories, and there were several entry points on the second floor, with the most promising being an outdoor deck that provided access to sliding-glass doors and another window. Beneath the deck was a basement door with a single-cylinder deadbolt. On the opposite end of the house was a segmented garage door.

Addie adjusted her bright orange safety vest and yellow hard hat. "Now what?"

"We pick the backdoor's lock." Sebastian pulled a tin container from his baggy pirate pants. "The tools of the trade. No good detective leaves home without 'em." He opened the lid. "Dang."

"What's wrong?" Bennett asked.

"These are mints. I must have left the lockpicks at home." He offered up the tin. "Want one?"

Bennett helped himself, but Addie said, "No thanks."

"Go ahead, take one."

"I don't like mints."

"Trust me." He shook the tin. "Take one. Maybe two."

Addie wrinkled her nose at the chimp's veiled insult. But she took a mint to be safe.

"Looks like it'll have to be the deck," Sebastian said. He stepped back and appraised the situation, sizing up the wooden support pillars. "Sturdy. Shouldn't be a problem at all."

"That's good," Addie said.

"Okay, up you go."

"What?"

"Start climbing."

"You're a monkey! Monkeys climb trees. It's what they do."

"Does it look like I'm dressed for climbing?" Sebastian was a right proper swashbuckler in a puffy calico shirt, black velvet vest, vertically striped pantaloons, and heavy cavalier boots. "I'm a pirate. I sail the seven seas. Bennett is a cowboy. He rides horses. You're a construction worker. Construction workers climb ladders and poles and all sorts of things. Hey, this is the life you chose."

"You made me be the construction worker!"

"It's not even that high. And there's no way he locked that window. Just slip through there and then come down and let us in the basement door."

"You know, my friend Jenny's family has a house key hidden in a fake rock in her backyard just in case they ever get locked out. Maybe Mitch has a key hidden somewhere."

"Bennett and I will be right here the whole time. Even if you fall, we'll catch you."

Addie looked up at the deck, which seemed higher than the clouds. "Are you sure?"

"Positive."

"You better catch me."

"Of course we will. Right, Bennett?"

"Right."

Addie reluctantly wrapped her arms and legs around the wooden pillar—her work gloves and rugged blue jeans protecting against potential splinters—and began to inch her way upward like a yellow-helmeted caterpillar.

"You might want to speed it up a bit," Sebastian said. "We don't have all day."

"I'm going as fast as I can."

"Just pretend you're a monkey."

"You are a monkey!"

While Addie continued her slow but steady advancement, Sebastian, already bored out of his mind, said to Bennett, "So…sixth grade coming up, huh?"

"Yeah."

"You nervous?"

"A little."

Addie called out, "This isn't so bad. I'm getting the hang of it."

"I never went to school," Sebastian said.

"How'd you get so smart?"

"TV."

"Mom doesn't like us watching too much TV."

"There's no such thing as too much TV."

Addie's improved technique had her within reach of the deck's floor. She stretched to get the fingertips of her right hand on the ledge. "Guys, I did it!"

"I should probably have a talk with your mother," Sebastian said to Bennett. "Not watching enough TV can really screw up a kid. I'd recommend at least eight or ten hours a day, more on weekends. You should really—" Something near the basement door caught the chimp's eye. "Does that flowerpot seem weird to you?"

Bennett followed Sebastian under the deck to investigate. Addie was in the process of pulling herself up on the deck's railing when she saw them passing beneath her. She looked down to see where they were going and lost her footing.

"Looks normal to me," Bennett said.

Sebastian crouched next to the red clay pot and poked its barren, dried-out soil with his finger. "But why is it here? Mitch clearly didn't care for beautifying his home. And this dirt hasn't been watered in ages."

Addie, now hanging by her fingertips from the deck, shouted, "Where are you, guys? Get over here!"

Sebastian and Bennett were still enthralled with the curious flowerpot. "You're doing great, Addie," Sebastian said. "Keep it up." He carefully tipped the flowerpot and peered underneath. "Would you look at that."

Addie's fingers were slipping. "Guys?"

Sebastian held up his discovery.

"A key!" Bennett said.

At that same moment, Addie's grip finally gave way, and she fell to the grass with a *thud*.

Sebastian inserted the key, and the basement door's lock clicked open. Without even looking back, he called out, "You can come down now, Addie. We found a key."

There was enough natural light from the open door to reveal an unfinished basement loaded with shelves and various plastic storage bins. "Looks like Mitch was a bit of a pack rat," Sebastian said. The switch just inside the door still worked, and fluorescent bulbs illuminated two clear panels of a drop ceiling, bathing the dank basement in electric light. While the exterior walls were white masonry block, the interior walls on the right were exposed insulation and wooden studs, a further indication that Mitch wasn't much for home improvements. Sebastian and Bennett ventured into the stale, stagnant air, the *click-clacks* of their boots bringing life to the eerily silent tomb.

Bennett stayed as close as he could to his chimp leader. "Feels weird being in a dead guy's house."

"All part of the job. But there's no reason to be afraid. Nothing in here can hurt us."

From behind them, Addie hollered, "Monkey!"

Sebastian and Bennett turned to see an unhinged construction worker huffing and puffing in the doorway.

"Well, almost nothing," Sebastian whispered. "Addie, my dear, how lovely of you to join us. I take it you made it down safely, no?"

Addie marched up to the chimp and poked him in the chest. "You were supposed to catch me."

Sebastian staggered backwards, trying to distance himself from the advancing Addie. "You fell?"

"Yes, I fell!" More angry poking. "I could've broke my neck because of you."

Bennett stepped between them to spare Sebastian further bruising. "Sorry, sis. We got distracted by the key. But I know Sebastian is really sorry too. Right, Sebastian?"

The chimp detective massaged his aching chest. "Yes, of course."

"That doesn't sound like an apology," Addie said.

"What do you want me to say?"

"Oh, I don't know, how about the words 'I'm sorry'?"

"Fine." Sebastian stood tall and cleared his throat. "Addie, I'm sorry you didn't break your neck."

"Apology accep—hey!" She drew back her fist. "You're gonna get it now, Monkey."

Bennett snared his sister around the waist to stop her from pummeling the chimp. However, her fitful outburst was still enough to startle Sebastian, and he stumbled into one of the shelves, dislodging a box and spilling its contents across the floor. Addie quit struggling when she noticed the scattered photographs.

"Hey, that's Jill Johnson."

Bennett put her down, and Addie's anger toward her chimp tormentor vanished, now replaced with equally intense curiosity. She knelt and picked up one of the photos. The image showed an attractive woman with long, straight auburn hair hugging Mitch Mayhem. The photo seemed to have been a selfie taken in the woods somewhere, as there were plenty of trees and a waterfall in the background.

"Who's Jill Johnson?" Sebastian asked.

Addie pointed to the woman in the photo. "Her. But why is she with Mitch?"

"Jill is the KCW women's champion," Bennett said. "She's a dentist."

"That's her gimmick?" Sebastian asked.

"And her real job. Think she could be involved in this?"

"Never trust a dentist," Addie said. She passed the photo to Sebastian and started going through the box's other contents.

"So, this was Mitch, huh?" Sebastian said. "Looks more like a waffle house cook than a wrestler." He passed the photo to Bennett. "Do you know what he did when he wasn't wrestling?"

"Heard he quit to try and be a writer, but that didn't work out. Before that, I think he used to sell insurance. But this photo is a few years old at least. Mitch looked a lot older than this the last time we saw him."

"Yeah," Addie said. "Looked like a hobo who lost his beans. There's a bunch of pictures of Jill in here. They must have been dating."

"Considering that these are old photos boxed away in the basement," Sebastian said, "I would venture to say that the relationship ended a while ago. Yet Mitch must have remained fond of her, or why keep the memories?"

"Seems like he had lots of memories," Addie said. She fanned out more photos, each one depicting Mitch with a different woman.

"He certainly kept busy. Do you recognize any of them?"

"Nope."

After cleaning up the photos and returning the box to its proper shelf, the trio of detectives inspected the numerous storage bins and found some old wrestling gear, books (true crime, thrillers, and mysteries), trading cards (hockey and football), comics (various publishers, including independents), DVDs (mostly horror films), and

CDs (grunge and alternative rock). While they certainly had a better idea of who Mitch was, they learned nothing that could indicate his murderer.

With the basement exhausted, they headed upstairs, which consisted of a living room, a bedroom, an office, a bathroom, and a kitchen. Sebastian wanted to save the living room for last, as Detective Carter had told him that was where the murder took place, so they began in the bathroom.

"If you want to learn about someone, always check the bathroom," Sebastian said. "Medicine cabinets hold many secrets."

"What's in your medicine cabinet, Monkey?" Addie asked.

"Why?"

"No reason."

"No, really, what did you hear?"

"Geez Louise, Monkey. Calm down."

Sebastian fixed Addie with a suspicious stare and then half-heartedly rummaged through the cabinets beneath the bathroom sink. Finding nothing, he hopped up on the sink and swung his boots into the basin so he could sit comfortably. Sebastian checked himself out in the medicine cabinet mirror, which was spotted with toothpaste splatter and water streaks, and seemed enamored with the fetching angle of his silk headscarf. "I do make a dashing pirate." He opened the cabinet and inspected its contents.

"Vitamins, anti-itch cream, antibiotic ointment, black hair dye."

"Mitch dyed his hair?" Addie said.

"Apparently."

"I didn't know men dyed their hair."

Sebastian forced a laugh. "Yeah, what kind of a man would dye his hair? Pretty crazy if you ask me." He glanced at his two companions, as if confirming whether they doubted his sincerity, and then quickly returned to rifling through the medicine cabinet. "More vitamins—no, wait, these aren't vitamins." Sebastian pulled out three prescription pill bottles. "What did you say that Jill woman's last name was?"

"Johnson," Bennett said.

"Now why do you suppose Dr. Johnson wrote Mitch prescriptions for pain medicine?"

"Could have hurt himself wrestling."

"Then why go to a dentist?"

Addie suggested, "Maybe he had a tooth pulled?"

"Must have been a persistent tooth." Sebastian turned the bottles so they could see the labels. "Refills on each. Seems our Mitch may have had a problem."

"This whole thing seems pretty fishy," Bennett said. "Why would Jill be giving him pills?"

Addie shook her head. "Never trust a dentist."

Satisfied with his efforts in the bathroom, Sebastian conducted a cursory inspection of the bedroom and found nothing of significance, other than Mitch's questionable choice of bedding. Who uses T-shirts for pillowcases? Next up was the office, a small room with an L-shaped desk that held a video game console and a gaming monitor. There was no hint of a laptop, cell phone, or tablet device, as the cops no doubt confiscated them as part of their investigation. Sebastian was rifling through a desk drawer—uncovering nothing more than a checkbook with one voided check and billing statements showing a considerable amount of credit card debt—when Addie piped up.

"I'm hungry."

Sebastian continued to search the desk drawers. "I'm not."

"That's because you ate a whole box of cookies before we left."

"There are plenty of cookies in the car."

"But I'm hungry now."

Sebastian spun the desk chair around and looked at Bennett. "Are you hungry?"

"A little."

"This is why I never had kids."

"Sure, that's why," Addie said.

"What's that supposed to mean?"

"Nothin'."

Sebastian exited into the hall, and Addie and Bennett followed. "Where you going?" she said.

"The kitchen."

"We can't eat a dead guy's food."

"He's certainly not going to need it."

Mitch's kitchen was like the rest of the house, neglected but serviceable. The side-by-side refrigerator, decorated with an assortment of restaurant menus and concert flyers held in place by Pittsburgh Penguins magnets, was the perfect match for the cheap plywood cabinets, laminated countertops, and warped linoleum flooring. Sebastian opened the refrigerator, and Addie and Bennett packed in behind him to see what offerings it held.

"That's it?" Addie said. "Olives, mustard, and Pepsi?"

Sebastian handed her the jar of mustard. "Enjoy."

"I can't eat mustard for lunch."

"Is there no end to your complaining?" He opened the freezer side. "Here." He pulled out a box of frozen waffles and handed them each one.

The kids studied the ice-encrusted breakfast treats. Addie said, "Aren't you gonna cook them for us?"

"Think of them as waffle freezer pops." He tossed the box back into the freezer and slammed the door, causing the attached menus to flutter.

"Hey, wait a second," Bennett said. He flipped up some of the menus to reveal a paper stamped with Dean Plumbing in the bottom right corner. "That's Mad Mike's company."

Sebastian plucked the paper free from its magnet. "It's an overdue bill for $827.32. And the original billing date was five months ago. This Dean chap is the hardcore wrestler, correct?"

"Yeah," Addie said, "I'm surprised he didn't bleed on the bill. A good sneeze will open up his forehead."

"Could he have killed Mitch over the money?" Bennett said.

Sebastian folded up the bill and put it in his pocket. "Seems unlikely. But certainly something to bring up when we interview Mr. Dean. Now eat your waffles before they get warm."

The lone remaining room to investigate was the living room, which is where the murder had occurred. Bennett pointed to a misshapen brown splotch on the tan carpeting. "What's that?"

"Oh, Mitch probably spilled some chocolate sauce or something," Sebastian said.

Addie gave up trying to gnaw through her waffle. "Don't lie, Monkey. That's Mitch's brains."

Bennett's eyebrows jumped, and he stepped back, bracing himself against the wall.

"It's not his brains," Sebastian said. "Quit scaring your brother."

"Then what is it, smart guy?"

"It's just…a little dried blood is all."

"Yeah, with bits of brain in it."

Bennett pressed the cold waffle to his forehead and slid his way down the wall. "I'll just be over here if you need me."

"Hang in there, buddy," Sebastian said. "We'll be done in a minute. But the stain is a vital clue because it tells us where Mitch was when he was struck. The room has a sofa and a recliner, and judging by the location of the mounted television, the recliner was no doubt Mitch's seat of choice. Had he been napping in the chair when the killer sneaked in and hit him, the blood stain would be on the chair. But it's not. It's in the center of the room."

Addie plopped into the recliner. "So, Mitch was standing when he was hit."

"Correct. Now, why would he be standing?"

"Maybe he heard the killer and came out here to confront him?" Bennett said, still looking green around the gills.

"Perhaps." Sebastian walked over to a bookshelf that displayed numerous wrestling awards and trophies. Some were wooden plaques with engraved nameplates, others standing trophies with gold-plated wrestlers posing atop heavy marble bases. Performer of the Year. Male Wrestler of the Year. Match of the Year. Mitch seemed popular. He picked up one of the trophies. "Detective Carter said that the murder weapon was an award similar to this one. Had the killer broken in and Mitch confronted him, would the killer come all the way over here to the bookshelf and choose one of the awards as a weapon?"

Addie tapped her rock-hard waffle on a small drink table positioned next to the recliner. "He didn't know these were in the freezer."

Sebastian returned the trophy to the shelf. "No, I believe Mitch invited the killer into his home. It was someone he knew and trusted. They were having a discussion. Things got heated. An argument ensued."

Addie stood from the recliner and acted out Sebastian's commentary, pantomiming a verbal dispute complete with shaking fist and wild gesticulations.

"There were no signs of struggle," Sebastian said. "None of the other awards were disturbed on the shelf, no lamps turned over, no bruising or scratches on Mitch's face. And remember, the blow was to the back of the head. He probably told the killer to get out."

Addie pointed to the door.

"But when Mitch turned to lead the way," Sebastian said, "the killer grabbed a trophy and struck in the heat of the moment."

Addie swung her waffle.

Bennett slowly climbed to his feet. "It was someone Mitch knew and trusted. Someone who had been arguing with him. And someone really strong."

"Sounds like Daddy," Addie said, frowning.

"Sure, but don't get discouraged," Sebastian said. "Things are seldom what they seem. People always misinterpret Occam's razor to mean that the simplest solution is always right, but that could not be further from the truth."

"What's Occam's razor?" Bennett asked.

Addie laughed. "What a dope. Can you believe he doesn't know what Occam's razor is?"

"What is it?" Sebastian said.

Addie held up her hand, fingers spread. "That's the one with five blades for a closer shave."

Sebastian rubbed his forehead as if warding off a migraine. "Occam's razor is a philosophical tool for evaluating theories, and it suggests that the simplest solution is always preferred. The common example most people give to illustrate the point is that if you hear hooves, think horses not zebras. That's all fine and dandy until you're run over by a pack of zebras. Do you understand what I'm saying?"

Bennett nodded, but Addie still seemed a little confused. "So… a zebra did it?"

"Let's try again," Sebastian said. "Just because it looks like a duck and quacks like a duck doesn't necessarily mean it's a duck."

"Ohhhhh, okay. A duck did it."

Sebastian pointed to Addie's frozen waffle. "Can I see that?"

Addie dutifully handed it over, only to have Sebastian stick it in her mouth, making her look like a puppy chewing a frisbee.

"We've learned all we can here," Sebastian said. "Now, we begin our interviews."

Bennett asked, "Who's first?"

"We'll start with Dean. Then I want to talk to the guy who owns the promotion and maybe that journalist fella who gives out all the wrestling awards. Time to rattle some cages. Turn up the heat. See who cracks." Sebastian flipped down his pirate eyepatch. "This is when it gets fun."

CHAPTER NINE

After the trio changed back into their regular clothes, they headed toward Dean Plumbing, with Addie and Bennett delighting in a nutritious lunch of Pioneer Scout cookies along the way.

"So, this Dean's a hardcore wrestler?" Sebastian said. "Barbed wire, thumb tacks, and all that?"

"Yeah," Addie said from the back seat, her mouth full of cookie. "Can't make it through a match without bleeding."

"Sounds like a rough customer."

"Biggest phony in the business. He's only tough to internet nerds who don't know what a real tough guy is."

"I don't know," Bennett said. "Seems pretty tough to me."

"Because you're an internet nerd. You should have seen it, Monkey. A couple months back, Dean was supposed to have an exploding ring match. Had the ropes wrapped in barbed wire and everything. But when the ring was supposed to explode, nothing happened. Just a couple sparklers went off. It was hilarious."

"You actually wanted the ring to explode?"

"Yeah, I did."

"But they couldn't have the ring actually explode," Bennett said. "People would get hurt."

"Hey, if you say the ring's gonna explode, you better make the ring explode. Dean ended up looking like a joke. He was selling it like a bomb went off, and it was a big dud. So funny."

"There really was supposed to be an explosion?" Sebastian asked.

"A bigger one than they had," Bennett said. "There were some more fireworks and stuff, but they never went off."

Addie jammed another chocolate-chip cookie in her mouth. "So, so funny."

Dean Plumbing was located in the Hadleyburg Shopping Plaza, which consisted of a dozen different businesses horseshoed around a large parking lot. The offerings included a Dollar Store, a Save-A-Lot grocery store, a Chinese restaurant, and a dry cleaner. Dean's one-window storefront was positioned between a pizza joint and a tanning salon. There were plenty of available parking spots. Shopping in downtown Hadleyburg had seen better days, with the local economy only slightly livelier than Mitch Mayhem. Sebastian pulled Ol' Blue next to a white van that had Dean Plumbing emblazoned on the side in bold red letters, along with contact information and the slogan Tougher Than Tough. A cartoon wrench with bulging biceps supported the claim.

The trio exited the car and walked up to the front window of the establishment. Inside, a burly gentleman in a green work shirt, its rolled-up sleeves exposing thick forearms, sat behind a desk eating a sandwich. His hunched posture, expansive forehead, reddish-brown beard, and tousled hair made him resemble a woebegone orangutan.

"That him?" Sebastian asked.

"Yeah," Addie said. "He wrestles even worse than he looks."

Bennett hid behind his sister. "Are you sure we have to interview him?"

"Quit being a scaredy cat. Besides, you've seen how he punches. We've got nothing to worry about."

Sebastian patted the right pocket of his smoking jacket. "If it puts your mind at ease, I took the precaution of loading up on weapons while I was putting away out disguises."

"The ninja stars!" Addie said, hopping up and down. "Lemme see, lemme see!"

"Not now. But rest assured, Mr. Dean will not be giving us any trouble."

"I hope he does." Addie swung her arm as if throwing a baseball. "I want to see him get ninjaed right between the eyes."

"Let's hope it doesn't come to that. Are you sure he won't recognize you?"

"Nah, Daddy never lets us get near him."

"Okay, then I need you to listen up, because it's time for your next lesson in being detectives: undercover work."

"Do we need disguises again?" Bennett asked.

"Not this time. But we will be disguising our true intentions. If we were to go in there and say we're detectives investigating the murder of Mitch Mayhem, he probably wouldn't tell us anything, or he might even get angry and throw us out. Thus, we must trick him into believing we're potential customers. That will get his guard down. Then I'll slip in a few subtle questions about the murder, and before he even realizes it, we'll have all the information we need."

"What do we have to do?"

"Nothing. I'll come up with a cover story, and you two just follow my lead. Got it?"

"Whatever, Monkey," Addie said. "Just have them ninja stars ready."

The three detectives entered Dean Plumbing to the sound of a jingling bell. The noise was enough to get Dean to look up from his phone, and he stared at them with the blank, lifeless eyes of one who has seen or done horrendous deeds. His face had the varicosed, ruddy complexion that resulted from a diet of equal parts red meat, alcohol, and more alcohol. He put down his sandwich, wiped some ketchup from his mouth with a calloused hand, and grunted, "Hey."

"Good afternoon, sir," Sebastian said. Addie was on his heels, but Bennett lagged behind, still reluctant to get close to the feral Dean. "My name is Percival Peabody, and I am the director of the Hadleyburg Home for Wayward Children. Sometimes children get lost, and when they do, it's up to us to smack 'em back in line. These are two of my many charges, Debbie and Bobby. And we are in the market for a plumber."

Dean looked to Addie and Bennett. "That's a talking monkey, right?"

While Bennett was too scared to respond, Addie nodded confirmation.

"Good." Dean took a swig of his Iron City bottle. "Thought I might have to give up drinking. Why you need a plumber?"

Sebastian patted Addie on the head. "Little Debbie here clogged the upstairs toilet something awful." Addie's cheeks almost got as red as Dean's. "I told her to quit eating chili for breakfast, but she never listens. Now I'm afraid we might have to redo the works. Toilets. Pipes. The whole megillah. Would you be capable of handling such a project?"

"Shouldn't be a problem."

"Is this a one-man operation? Or do you have other plumbers on staff?"

"I've always got at least two vans out on the road. But I usually just handle the office stuff these days. Only go out when needed."

"It certainly is a fine place you have here." Sebastian noted a row of framed wrestling photos on the wall. He pointed to the nearest one. "That you?"

"Yeah, I wrestle for KCW on the weekends."

Sebastian meandered from the desk to get a better look at the picture, which featured a blood-soaked Dean stretched between the ropes and his opponent digging what appeared to be a pizza cutter into his forehead. "Seems like good, wholesome family fun. Maybe we'll take some of the wayward children to the next event. Would you like that, Bobby?"

Bennett was still frozen with terror at being so close to Dean. Only an elbow from Addie sparked an, "Uh-huh."

"KCW?" Sebastian said. "I think I heard about that on the news. Wasn't one of you wrestler chaps just murdered?"

"Yeah," Dean said, his voice a rough patch of gravel. "So how many toilets we talking here? One? Two?"

"Oh, probably twelve. Debbie does love her chili. Did you know the guy who got killed?"

"Used to be tag partners."

"Sorry for your loss."

"Don't mention it. We weren't that close."

"But you were partners."

"That was years ago." Dean took another bite of his chipped-ham sandwich. "He was actually a jerk."

"Seemed to be pretty popular with the fans."

"Couldn't wrestle his way out of a wet paper bag."

"But wasn't he the champion? Must have been pretty good."

"Yeah, at kissing up to the boss."

"That Tony Katsaros fella? Heard about him on the news too. Seems nice enough."

"Spoiled little rich kid. No business running a wrestling promotion, but daddy's money lets him do whatever he wants."

"Mitch didn't deserve to be champ?"

"Far be it from me to speak ill of the dead, but Mitch was washed. You gotta understand, there's a lot of politics in wrestling. A lot."

"Is that right?" Sebastian said, feigning ignorance. "Had no idea it was so cutthroat."

"Everybody protects their spot. Mitch was just better at it than most. He wasn't scared to throw his weight around. And the boss loved him, so Mitch always got what he wanted."

"How'd that go over with the other wrestlers?"

"How do you think?" Dean took a swig of beer. The alcohol seemed to soothe his raw nerves. "But, hey, no one said life was fair. The best wrestlers aren't always champs."

"Like Bonecrusher," Addie said.

Dean turned his dead eyes to Addie. "What's that?"

"Bonecrusher should be champ."

"Bonecrusher?" Dean laughed. "He's a glorified jobber. Besides, tough to win the belt from a prison cell."

Addie slammed her fists on the desk, causing Bennett to jump with fright. "Take it back."

"Take what back?"

"Bonecrusher is not a jobber!"

"Geez, what got into you? You know Bonecrusher or somethin'?"

Sebastian carefully removed Addie's fists from Dean's desk. "Forgive Debbie. She is an excitable one. Probably why she has so much stomach trouble."

"Listen," Dean said, "Bonecrusher's a good hand. I like the guy. But he's not championship material is all."

"And you are?" Addie said.

"Now, Debbie," Sebastian said. "These are hardly the manners we teach you at the orphanage."

Dean held up three gnarled fingers. "Three-time champ."

Addie scoffed. "Three-time loser is more like it."

Dean leaned forward and pointed at her. "Watch your mouth."

"Or what? You gonna kill me like you killed Mitch?"

"What are you talking about?"

Addie pilfered the overdue plumbing bill from Sebastian's unguarded left pocket and threw it across the desk at Dean. "Read it and weep."

Dean unfolded the paper, the tapestry of scar tissue across his razor-carved forehead conveying confused worry. "Where'd you get this?"

"Admit it," Addie said. "Mitch owed you money and wouldn't pay, so you killed him."

"Are you nuts? Why would I kill someone over eight hundred bucks?"

"So, he did owe you the money?" Sebastian asked.

"He had a pipe burst last winter. Said he wasn't happy with the work. But he was just being a big baby, like usual, and didn't want to pay. But we talked things over, and he was gonna make good first of the month. The whole thing was settled."

Addie folded her arms across her chest. "Likely story."

"What's it to you anyway? You cops or somethin'?"

"We're detectives," Addie said. "And we know you killed Mitch."

Sebastian waved off Addie's accusation. "That's only partly true. Yes, I am a detective. And my two assistants and I are investigating the murder of Mitch Mayhem because we have reason to believe that Bonecrusher is innocent. But my overzealous colleague got a bit carried away. We do not think that you killed him. We're just trying to track down potential leads, like that overdue bill there."

Dean, measuring at least six-three and well north of two hundred pounds, shoved back from the desk and stood. "I don't like detectives poking their noses in my business." He stared at Bennett, and a flicker of recognition dawned. "Hey, Poindexter. You look familiar. I know you?"

Bennett said, "Maybe we should go…."

"Listen to the pencil-necked geek. Scram."

"There's no need for name calling," Sebastian said, "And you know, your reaction to all this is making you seem pretty guilty."

"You got three seconds before I throw you out."

"We're not scared of you," Addie said.

"One."

Bennett attempted to pull his fellow detectives toward the door. "Let's go already."

Dean cracked his knuckles. "Two."

"I should warn you," Sebastian said, "I will defend myself if provoked."

"Three."

Dean started around the desk.

Addie shouted, "Let him have it, Monkey!"

Quicker than an Old West gunslinger, Sebastian reached into the pocket of his smoking jacket and hurtled a handful of projectiles at the onrushing madman. However, the missiles, in no way reminiscent of throwing stars, merely bounced off Dean's chest and did little to slow his charge. The perturbed plumber seized Sebastian by the lapels of his smoking jacket with one hand, toted him to the front door, and casually chucked him outside like a sack of spuds. He then held the door open for Addie and Bennett, who hastened to join their fallen leader.

Sebastian was stretched out on the parking lot pavement like a simian speed bump. Bennett hurried over to help him up. "You okay, Sebastian?"

The great chimp detective shook out the cobwebs and dusted off his fancy trousers. "That could have gone better."

Addie showed little concern for his health. "Where were the ninja stars?"

"I don't have ninja stars. I use perfectly legal, non-lethal weapons that can be deployed in any situation whenever necessary. How was I to know that big oaf would be immune to such tactics?"

"What were those things anyway?" Bennett asked.

"Roasted chickpeas."

"You threw roasted chickpeas at him?" Addie said.

"Have you ever had a roasted chickpea? They're very hard."

"You're a dummy."

"Oh, really? I wasn't the dummy who blew our cover. Things were going great until you screwed it up."

"He shouldn't have said that about Daddy."

"People are always going to say stupid things. It's what they do. You can't let it bother you. I mean, he called Bennett a 'pencil-necked geek,' and you don't see him crying about it."

Bennett lowered his head. "Did kind of hurt my feelings."

"It's like I'm working with children."

"We are children," Addie said.

"No, you're detectives. And detectives must always remain calm under pressure. We have to go interview that promoter guy next. What's going to happen if he calls you a loud-mouthed little twerp who never shuts up? Or what if he says your head is way too big for your body? I don't even care if he points out that your ears are weird and make you look like a walking science project, you can't get emotional. Got it?"

Addie reached up to inspect her ears. "My ears are weird?"

"Maybe not *weird* exactly…."

"Seriously, Monkey, what's wrong with my ears?"

The chimp detective reached into his pocket and produced a peace offering. "Chickpea?"

Addie slapped away the proffered bean and stomped back to the car, showing that she still needed to work on controlling her emotions.

CHAPTER TEN

"Did you say he owns the company?" Sebastian asked.

"Tiny's dad owns it," Addie said from the back seat. "Tiny just goofs off and cashes checks."

"What is it they do exactly?"

"They make the little ditties for those thingies."

"Oh, well that explains it."

"They make the plastic caps for tire valves," Bennett said, providing a more accurate description of the business endeavor.

"Thrilling."

"I guess we can't be undercover for this one though, huh? Tony knows us."

Sebastian parked Ol' Blue in front of the office building. "He may know who you are, but he doesn't know why you're here. I'm your uncle. I'm helping my dear sister watch you kids while your father is in jail. I'm also in the market for some new plastic caps for my tire valves. The two of you suggested I come here because you're so fond of Tony."

"But I hate Tiny," Addie said. "He's a spaz."

"That's not nice."

"Wait until you meet him. He has no business running a wrestling promotion, and his booking is terrible."

"Just pretend. If he thinks you like him, it will put him at ease, and we'll probably get more information out of him."

"Whatever. What should we call you?"

"Like I said, I'm your uncle."

"But what's your name?"

"Just call me Sebastian."

"You shouldn't use your real name."

Sebastian turned in his seat to look back at Addie. "What could it possibly matter?"

"Doesn't seem very professional is all." Addie hit Bennett's seat. "Do you think he should use his real name?"

"A fake name might be better."

"Fine," Sebastian said. "And what would you like to call me?"

"Gary," Addie said without the slightest hesitation.

Sebastian shuddered at the thought. "What? Do I really look like a Gary to you?"

"What's wrong with Gary?"

"It's so blah. Give me something with a bit more character. Something stronger, more masculine. Like Victor. Or Augustus."

"You look more like a Gary."

"How is that even possible?"

"What about Carl?" Bennett said.

"That's worse. You know what? Just forget the whole thing. Call me Sebastian, and that's that."

"Fine," Addie said. "You're the boss."

The trio piled out of Ol' Blue and made their way into the building's lobby. Katsaros Enterprises was on the sixth floor, and when they opened the door to the company's offices, they met a young receptionist with short blonde hair who quickly put aside her cell phone.

"Can I help you?" She didn't seem the least surprised to welcome two children and a chimp.

Addie stepped in front of Sebastian and provided introductions. "Hi, I'm Addie. This is my brother Bennett, and this here is our uncle Gary Carl. We'd like to talk to Tiny, please."

The young woman looked confused. "I don't know anyone named Tiny…."

"I'm sorry," Sebastian said, quietly fuming over Addie's choice of names for him. "Did my stupid, stupid niece say Tiny? She meant Tony. I believe his father owns the company."

The young woman's confusion only worsened. "You want to talk to Tony? No one ever wants to talk to Tony."

"Yes, I desperately need to order a massive amount of plastic caps for my tire valves, and Tony is the only man I trust for the job."

She looked at the reception desk's telephone. "He doesn't even have an extension. Like, seriously, you want to talk to the kid, not the father? Are you sure?"

Sebastian, Addie, and Bennett nodded in unison.

"Okay." She pushed herself back from the desk and stood, the reluctance clear in her movements. "Follow me, I guess."

She led them down a short hallway and knocked on a door marked with an engraved nameplate that read "Tony Katsaros, Executive Vice President." The first knock went unanswered. "He's probably busy working." She took a deep breath and knocked again before slowly opening the door. "Mr. Katsaros?"

Tony Katsaros, Executive Vice President, never heard the knocks because he was otherwise occupied smashing wrestling figures together in a toy ring. His ongoing commentary, complete with crowd chants and sound effects, ceased only when the receptionist loudly cleared her throat and rapped on his desk.

Tony glanced up from his playset, his mop of curly black hair and large, bulging eyes making him look like a malnourished poodle.

"Mr. Katsaros, you have some potential clients who would like to meet with you."

"Thanks, toots," Addie said. "We'll take it from here. Hey, Tony, it's me, Addie Pajakowski, Bonecrusher's kid. You remember my brother Bennett. And this is our uncle Gary Carl. He wants to buy some little ditties for his tires."

"Oh, hey, Addie," Tony said. He dropped his wrestling figures and pushed aside the toy ring like the true professional he was. "I'll handle this, Ashley. But thank you for bringing this important business matter to my attention."

Before leaving, Ashley pulled Bennett aside and whispered, "Is your uncle a monkey?"

"No, ma'am."

"That's what I figured. I mean, a talking monkey would—"

"He's a chimpanzee."

She left without further comment.

"I'd ask you guys to sit down," Tony said, "but Dad took away all my chairs. There was…an incident. But hey, I hope you kids know I think your father's innocent. Sure it's all just a big misunderstanding. How have you and your mom been doing?"

"We're hanging in there," Addie said. "Uncle Gary Carl has been a big help."

"Love the name, by the way," Tony said to Sebastian. "Very unusual."

"Yes, my parents were idiots."

"I'd like to help you, but we don't actually sell the caps here from the offices. You can get them at any of the local auto stores, or you can order them online from our website."

"LittlePlasticDittiesForThingies.com?" Addie said.

"No, it's actually…um…you know what? I'll just have Ashley write it down for you on the way out. I'm not really good with stuff like that. I'm more of a big-picture guy. That's probably why I'm such a great promoter."

"That's right," Sebastian said. "When we were driving over here, Addie and Bennett told me you're the owner of the wrestling promotion where their dad works."

"Tony's the best booker in the business," Addie said. She followed up with an exaggerated wink to Sebastian, just to let him know that she was playing her part.

"Not to brag," Tony said, the pride obvious on his highly punchable face, "but the Squared Circle named me its Booker of the Year."

It was now Sebastian's turn to play dumb. "And the *booker* is the person who makes the matches, right?"

"Yep." Tony held up a leather-bound notebook. "This is where the magic happens. I plan all the shows right here. Everything handwritten just like in the old territory days."

"That sounds pretty neat. Would you mind if I take a look?"

"Please do. I love talking about this stuff."

The chimp detective returned Addie's deliberate wink, letting his associates know that things were going according to plan.

Tony tried to open his trusty notebook but fumbled it a few times before it hit the floor. Once he got his butterfingers under control, he opened the notebook like a calendar, the pages flipping up and down instead of left to right. "Here's the card from our last show. I write with the page in landscape mode. That's how I do things now. Started a couple weeks ago, and it blew my mind. Changed everything. Anyway, I want to have nothing but bangers. No cool-off matches or ebbs and flows, just straight fire from the opening bell. Wanna know how you get a crowd hot? Open with a six-man tag match featuring Lenny Lambda and the Hickson Brothers. All gas, no brakes. Nonstop action. I mean, that's what fans want to see, right?"

"What about the finer points of storytelling and ring psychology?" Sebastian said.

"Oh, that's in there too. Don't you worry. We've got everything. Isn't that right, kids? Tell your uncle. There's no show better than a KCW show."

Addie nearly combusted from swallowing her fiery criticisms of his cockamamie booking. Just to be safe, Bennett clamped his hand over his sister's mouth and said, "My sister and I love your shows."

"Thanks, guys. That really means a lot. But, hey, Gary Carl, look here." He pointed at a line in the notebook. "In match two, we had Jill Johnson, our women's champ, defend her title against Penelope Hayes. Two of the best workers in the business. Jill retained by submission. Remember that, kids?"

Addie pulled Bennett's hand away just long enough to yell, "You always have Jill win, and it's getting—"

"Better and better each time," Bennett said, once more silencing his sister.

"Yeah, she's the best," Tony said. "I love her." He admired the little hearts he had drawn in the margins next to Jill's name before quickly glancing at Sebastian. "I mean, I respect her as a performer. She's a really good wrestler. Seriously, that's all I meant."

"I believe you," Sebastian said.

"Good." Tony returned to his notebook. In his baggy black tracksuit, he resembled an incompetent jewel thief, and he had the nervous energy and spastic movements of a precocious child whose mommy had given him too much money for the candy machine. "Match three featured Mad Mike Dean in a hardcore death match against Dutch Kincaid. So good. Have you ever seen Dean wrestle? He is one tough son of a gun."

"I don't know about that," Sebastian said. "I hear he picks on opponents much smaller than him, grabs them by the lapels of their ridiculously expensive silk smoking jackets when they're not looking, and then uses illegal maneuvers to claim victory before the fight's even truly begun."

"I've never booked a match like that."

"I'm just saying he seems like that kind of guy. Can't win a fair fight, so he cheats."

"Trust me, you do not want to cross Mad Mike."

"Yeah, yeah, sure, but what about the last match here." Sebastian pointed to the main event. "I see you have a line through this Manero fella's name, and you wrote in my brother-in-law, Bonecrusher. Was Manero supposed to wrestle Mitch?"

"That was the initial idea, but there was a bit of a problem backstage."

"What sort of problem?"

Addie stomped on Bennett's foot, causing him to yelp and release his grip on her mouth. She took the opportunity to shout, "Mitch being a crybaby."

"That's not true," Tony said, his eyes crackling with nervous energy. "Mitch was just very particular about what he wanted for his career. And he didn't feel that wrestling Manero at that point in time was the best possible option."

"Do you always let the talent call the shots?" Sebastian asked.

"Don't you worry. I'm the boss." Tony pulled up his big-boy pants. "What I say goes. It just so happens that I usually agreed with whatever Mitch wanted."

"How did Manero take getting bumped from the title match?"

"There were some hurt feelings, naturally. But a big part of my job is managing egos. Luckily, I'm really good at it." He locked eyes with Sebastian and, with solemn sincerity, said, "I was born to do this."

"Then why'd you have Mitch squash our dad?" Addie said. "You'd been doing a decent job of building him as a monster heel, and then you threw it all out the window."

"Again, that was more of a Mitch call, but I'm sure he had a long-term payoff in mind and never expected that your dad would—I mean, you know."

Sebastian said, "Will you be naming a new champion now that Mitch is gone?"

"Funny you should ask because I was just working on the card for this weekend. It's gonna be a special tribute show to Mitch. But since the championship has gone missing, I have to get another belt made, and it won't be ready in time to crown a new champ. Instead, the main event will be a tag team match featuring Lenny Lambda and one of the Hickson Brothers versus Mad Mike Dean and Vince Manero. This will be the first time Dean and Manero have ever tagged. And then the members of the winning team will eventually face each other for the world title. How great is that?"

"Eh, I don't know," Addie said.

"What do you mean?" Tony said, his voice cracking. "That's a great idea."

"Obviously, Mad Mike and Manero are gonna win, and it's just the whole 'can they coexist' storyline that's been done to death."

Tony seemed heartbroken. "You don't think the fans will like it?"

"Stupid ones might."

He turned to her brother in desperation. "Bennett?"

"Maybe this will be the one time that story works."

"Oh no, this is awful." Tony clamped his eyes shut in pained concentration, as if trying to mine a better idea from his feeble brain. "I need a good showing to win back the TV execs."

"TV execs?" Sebastian said.

"Yeah, I'm negotiating a deal with WPXI. Mitch's death has made us the hottest ticket in town, and I need to strike while the iron's hot." He jumped out of his seat and ran to the door. "Would you guys mind? I really have to get this card figured out."

Sebastian thanked Tony for his time and walked Addie and Bennett from the office. After the door shut, Addie looked at Sebastian. "Well?"

"What a spaz."

Just then, a large man in a fur-trimmed overcoat and bowler hat emerged from an office at the end of the hall. He had an impressive handlebar mustache, its deep black coloring with white wisps making it stand out like a skunk's tail against his olive skin. His herringbone suit was clearly tailored to fit his pear-shaped body, and his well-polished brown leather shoes sparkled. He tipped his hat to Addie, Bennett, and Sebastian.

Sebastian nudged Bennett. "Get a load of that guy. Brown shoes? It's like I'm the only one who knows how to dress these days."

"That's Tiny's dad," Addie said. "C'mon." She chased after him, with Bennett in hot pursuit.

Sebastian sighed. "No one said there would be running."

CHAPTER ELEVEN

"Ashley, I'll be at the club if anyone needs me," Mr. Katsaros said to the receptionist on his way through the lobby. "But make sure no one needs me."

"Certainly, Mr. Katsaros."

Addie and Bennett raced after their prey, with Sebastian trailing at a slightly accelerated stroll, and managed to catch the lobby door before it even had a chance to close behind Mr. Katsaros. The brother and sister fell in beside Tony's father at the elevator.

Addie tugged the sleeve of his overcoat. "Aren't you Tony's dad?"

Mr. Katsaros looked down at the little girl and smiled. "Oh, hello there. You know Tony?"

"Yeah, my name's Addie. This is my brother Bennett." She pointed to the late-arriving Sebastian, who was just making his way through the lobby door. "And he's our uncle Gary Carl."

Mr. Katsaros eyed Sebastian. "Have you ever been to Greece? You remind me of my uncle Yiorgos back in Corfu."

"Must be a handsome man," Sebastian said.

Addie mumbled "Doubt it" beneath her breath and then said, "We just had a meeting with Tony."

"Is that right?" The elevator doors opened, and Mr. Katsaros stepped aside to let his new friends enter first. "Say, that's a fine smoking jacket."

"Thank you," Sebastian said, stepping into the elevator. "Notice how it matches my shoes."

Mr. Katsaros joined them and pushed the button for the ground floor. The elevator doors slid shut, and they began to slowly descend. "Never known Tony to take meetings. Are you in the market for tire valve caps?"

"Actually, we were interested in his wrestling promotion," Sebastian said.

Mr. Katsaros laughed. "Should have known. That boy and his wrestling."

"Not a wrestling fan? We heard you were bankrolling the promotion."

"Oh, I suppose wrestling is as good as any other hobby, but unless you're making money, that's all it is. A hobby." The elevator came to a halt, and Mr. Katsaros once again motioned for Addie, Bennett, and Sebastian to go first. "It's nice that I get to watch my son enjoy his inheritance while I'm still alive, but at some point the faucet has to turn off. It's just bad business."

"Does Tony know this?"

"Believe me, he is aware," Mr. Katsaros said, chuckling the rest of the way to the parking lot. "But I really must be going. It was a pleasure meeting you all, and I hope your dealings with Tony prove fruitful."

He climbed into a black BMW and drove away with a friendly beep-beep of the horn.

"Sounds like Tony might not be a wrestling promoter much longer," Bennett said.

"And if he blamed Mitch for ruining his TV deal," Sebastian said, "that could be motive for murder. I think it's time we get some more information about Tony and his promotion."

Sitting once more behind the wheel of Ol' Blue, Sebastian planned the next step in their investigation.

"With the help of a secret database available to only elite private investigators, I will now obtain the home address of Steve Thacker, wrestling journalist." Sebastian's thumbs tapped away on his cell phone. "You'd be amazed at the information I can get on someone.

Once you reach a certain level of success, doors open up for you. Being a private investigator quits being a profession and is more like a brotherhood, a fraternity. I have connections all around the world, an ever-expanding network of contacts, including informants, forensic experts, and hired muscle, all just a click away. Most civilians don't even know this database exists, yet here you two are, about to witness a trade secret." Sebastian tapped the screen.

"What's the matter?" Bennett said.

"Wrong password. Must have missed a key. Let me just type it again…and…hmm. I know I typed it right that time."

"What's your password, Monkey?"

"I'm not going to tell you my password."

"I bet it's Banana."

"It's not Banana." Sebastian tried again. Still didn't work. He kept trying and failing.

"Banana1?" Addie said. "Banana2? Banana3? Banan—"

"Would you be quiet." Sebastian rubbed his eyes. "Gotta think. I know it's in there somewhere. Think, think, think."

"Is it your birthday?" Bennett said.

"No, it's not my birthday."

"What about your dad's birthday?" Addie said.

"Forget birthdays. I would never use a birthday as a password. Give me more credit than that."

"Does it have something to do with one of those old TV shows you were telling us about?" Bennett said.

"Don't think so. But it probably has something to—wait, I got it." Sebastian's thumbs were once again a blur. "In." He tapped his forehead. "Like a steel trap."

"What was it?" Addie said.

"Don't worry about it."

"Aw, c'mon, Monkey. It's just us. We won't tell anybody."

Sebastian murmured something.

"What? We didn't hear you."

"Banana7. But the important thing is that we're in. Now watch and learn how a true detective—"

"Found it," Bennett showed Sebastian his phone, which displayed Thacker's home address and extensive personal information.

"You're on the database too?"

"I just Googled it." He tapped the screen a few times and handed the phone to Sebastian. "And that's his website."

The featured free article was an editorial suggesting that Tony Katsaros make Lenny Lambda the next KCW champion. "Run-on sentences. Shameful syntax. A general disdain for basic grammar. Who pays to read this gibberish?"

"A bunch of dummies, that's who," Addie said.

"Hopefully he can use the money to buy some punctuation."

Further digging revealed that Thacker was sixty-four years old, a divorced father of two, and an accountant by trade. A lifelong wrestling fan, he started a wrestling newsletter as a hobby in the early 1980s, and he had a soft spot for the local promotion, championing it throughout its various incarnations and owners. Along with the online subscription website, he hosted a weekly podcast from a one-bedroom apartment in South Hadleyburg. And today, when he opened the front door of that very same apartment, he saw three smiling faces looking back at him.

"Good afternoon," Sebastian said with a slight bow. "My name is Sebastian Winthrop, and I—"

"Any relation to Leaping Lord Winthrop, the junior heavyweight champion of the Minnesota territory in 1956?"

Sebastian was a bit taken aback by the bizarre tangent. Thacker, despite his advanced age, looked properly jacked in a tight, tucked-in polo shirt and belted acid-washed jeans, a lifetime of weightlifting evident in his muscular physique. "I don't believe so, no."

"Similar gimmick," Thacker said. "He was a bit hairier, though."

"Yes, well, my colleagues and I are investigating the Mitch Mayhem murder and were wondering if you could help provide us with some background on the key players."

"What's to investigate? The police arrested Stanley Pajakowski."

"We have reason to believe that Mr. Pajakowski is innocent. Any help you could give would be greatly appreciated."

Thacker hesitated a moment, staring at Sebastian with cold gray eyes that had about as much spark as an unplugged toaster. "Not sure what I can do, but okay."

He withdrew into the apartment, not bothering to hold the door for his guests. Sebastian, Addie, and Bennett stepped inside and entered a wonderland of waste. Loose papers, overstuffed cardboard boxes, and discarded protein bar wrappers covered the entire floor. Wrestling posters, boasting such names as Mascaras, Kobashi, and Rikidozan, plastered the off-white walls. The room had one sofa, also buried beneath assorted debris, and two work desks on opposite walls, each sporting its own computer and avalanche of papers. A large window stretched between the two desks and provided enough light through its vertical hanging blinds to expose the true absurdity of the mindboggling mess.

Bennett whispered, "Mom would be so mad."

Sebastian kicked aside some crumpled paper to close the door. "Did you decorate this yourself or did you have a hurricane do it?"

"Hurricanes can't form inside apartments," Thacker said, with no hint of humor. He carefully maneuvered his way to the far desk, the neglected papers crinkling beneath his stocking feet, and settled into a swivel hair. "Have a seat."

"Where?" Addie said, in awe of the disaster zone.

"That's okay," Sebastian said. "We'll stand. Not sure we've all had our typhoid shots. But can you fill me in on Mitch's career? You must have been a fan, considering all the awards you gave him."

"Mitch was a trailblazer on the independent scene. He wasn't a natural athlete, but he was exceptional on the mic and could talk people into the building. He was a local legend for years until he decided to hang up his boots. But Tony Katsaros talked him out of retirement."

"How'd he convince him?"

"Money."

"It's undefeated. But from what I hear, Mitch said some harsh things about you after his last match."

"Did he?" Thacker said. "Don't remember."

"Sure you do," Addie said. "He called you a stooge."

"Actually," Bennett interjected, "he said you're a liar, and then he called the person who gives you your information a stooge. But it was implied that you were a stooge too."

"I'm a journalist," Thacker said. "Sometimes, my reporting upsets people."

"Good one," Addie said. "Okay, Mr. Big Important Journalist Guy, who's feeding you all your stories?"

"I can't reveal my sources."

"Because they don't exist."

"Not true. I have lots of sources."

"You make up stuff, and whenever you're wrong, you just say 'plans changed.' What a scam."

"Again, not true."

"Oh, if it's not true, then I guess you can write about it in your stupid newsletter, huh?"

Thacker squinted his beady eyes at Addie. "Who are you again?"

Addie returned the squint. "I'm your worst nightmare."

"She's everyone's worst nightmare," Sebastian said, "don't let it bother you. But how did the rest of the boys feel about Mitch wrestling again?"

"Most were excited."

"Most?"

"His troubled relationship with Mad Mike Dean is well documented. Manero was also less than enthused. Dean was supposed to drop the belt to Manero. Give him one final championship run. But when Mitch came back, plans chan—they went a different direction."

"Mitch have heat with anyone else backstage?"

"Clearly. I mean, Pajakowski murdered him."

Addie thrusted forward like a pint-sized pit bull. "He didn't do it!"

A startled Thacker flinched, and had his wheeled desk chair not been rooted in rubbish, he likely would have careened into the wall.

"Forgive my colleague," Sebastian said, patting the agitated Addie on the shoulder to calm her down. "She has a real passion for justice. But I heard Mitch was butting heads with Lenny Lambda and the Hickson Brothers."

"Oh, Lenny couldn't have killed Mitch. But had Lenny been murdered, Mitch would have been the prime suspect."

"Why's that?"

"Jealousy. Lenny is the best wrestler in the world."

Addie laughed. "Hilarious."

"Pardon me?"

"Oh, nothing. I just thought it was really, really funny when you said Lenny Lambda is the best wrestler in the world when he actually stinks."

Thacker sat bolt upright in his chair. "Lenny's the best."

"Says you."

"Says everyone with a brain."

"Then I guess that leaves you out."

Sebastian stepped between the two heated rivals and pointed to some cluttered shelving beneath the window that displayed five championship belts of varying designs and colors. "Hey, Bennett, look at those beauties."

"Did you win those?" Bennett asked.

Addie cackled again. "Yeah, right. He's never wrestled in his life."

Sebastian flexed his bicep to indicate Thacker's impressive arms. "You look big enough to have laced up the boots once or twice."

"Those are just a few of my favorite belts," Thacker said. "Replicas, of course. The real ones are locked away. I'm a wrestling historian and an avid collector, but I've never had the desire to actually wrestle."

"Yeah," Addie said, "why wrestle when you can just criticize those who do?"

"You don't have to be a whale to write Moby-Dick."

Addie squared up, her fists at the ready. "What did you call me?"

"Two desks, huh?" Sebastian said, desperate to change the subject. "Does someone else work here?"

"No."

Sebastian appeared perplexed by the unoccupied but equally chaotic workstation, unable to deduce its significance. The only differences were a fire extinguisher sitting in one corner—at least offering some protection from the entire room being a firetrap—and a cushioned metal folding chair as opposed to the more traditional office swivel chair. "Why two desks?"

"I like desks."

"You also like Lenny Lambda," Addie said, "and that's just as dumb."

"I'm not going to argue with you about this."

"Because you know you're wrong."

"Lenny is an artist."

"Some artist. Dude can't draw a dime."

"You're too young to understand the psychology of his matches."

"Oh, because you're soooooo smart. What's to understand? People pretend to hit him, and he pretends it hurts. Big whoop."

Sebastian once more tried to intervene. "Maybe we should all just take a deep breath and—"

"Lenny is objectively the best," Thacker said. "He has more five-star matches than anyone. And he's the only person to have two seven-star matches."

"You gave him those ratings!" Addie said.

Bennett cleared his throat. "You also probably shouldn't have gone over five stars. Pretty much ruined the established scale you had been using."

"My scale is a living thing, always growing and evolving."

Bennett slowly shook his head. "That doesn't make any sense."

Sebastian once again tried to calm the waters, but Addie shoved him out of the way.

"Nothing this dummy says makes any sense. He gave Daddy's match with Killer Carlson one star."

"Daddy?" The wrinkles in Thacker's forehead deepened. "Pajakowski's your father?"

"Yeah, he's our father. And he's a way better wrestler than Lenny will ever be."

"Your father has never had a single four-star match in his entire career."

"Because he's a real wrestler and doesn't do a bunch of meaningless moves and dopey flips like some stupid spot monkey." She quickly turned to Sebastian. "No offense, Monkey."

Sebastian shook off any possible insult. "None taken."

"Times have changed," Thacker said. "Your father's style of wrestling is outdated. Lenny is the future. Fans want high spots. They want flips and dives. They want fast action, not headlocks and rest holds."

"You just like Lenny and his brothers because they make you feel cool. I got news for you, bucko. You're not cool. And you're—"

Buzz. Buzz.

Addie reached into the pocket of her Pioneer Scout skirt and pulled out her phone. "Oh, great. It's NiNi." She pointed at Thacker. "I'm not done with you." She turned her back to the alleged wrestling journalist and answered the call. "What up, NiNi? Bennett and I were just…well, no, we're not, but— It wasn't so much a lie as…oh, just someone we know…I told Bennett it was a bad idea, but he—"

At the sound of his name, Bennett looked to Sebastian, panic-stricken.

"Okay, okay, calm down," Addie said. "Yes, NiNi…right away…okay, already. Yeah, yeah, yeah. I got it…no, I wasn't being…yes, NiNi…okay."

She ended the call and slipped the phone back into her pocket, the disappointment etched on her face.

"We gotta go."

CHAPTER TWELVE

Addie and Bennett, once again burdened with their respective backpacks, trudged up the steps to their grandmother's front porch, dreading the reception they were about to receive. Sebastian followed close behind, toting the cookie bag.

"Now remember, Monkey," Addie said upon reaching the front door, "NiNi is a crazy old lady. So try not to get her mad."

"Nothing to fear. Old people love me."

"You don't know NiNi. She's—"

"Addelynn Marie Pajakowski!" boomed a voice from inside the house, its echo complementing the terrifying thumps of fast-approaching footsteps. "Get in here right this minute and—"

When the front door ripped open, standing before Sebastian was not some decrepit spinster but a statuesque beauty with long, chestnut-brown hair, luscious curves, and legs that stretched higher than coconut trees. Her exquisite almond-shaped eyes were only enhanced by her bewitching eyeglasses, making her seem like a librarian with a particularly intriguing secret. This glorious woman, who made jeans and a sweatshirt dazzle like haute couture, immediately fell silent upon seeing the children and their mysterious companion. After a prolonged moment of befuddlement, she blurted out a single word: "Chimp."

"That's right, my dear," Sebastian said. "Lesser minds often confuse me with a common monkey. But I'm afraid there must be some mistake, because I was told that these children's grandmother lived here, not Helen of Troy."

NiNi continued to stare.

Sebastian passed the cookie bag off to Bennett and extended his hand. "Sebastian Winthrop."

NiNi shook Sebastian's hand like a mindless robot performing its programming. "Talking chimp."

Sebastian kissed her hand. "Charmed, I'm sure."

"Sebastian's a detective," Bennett said.

"Yeah, sorry about lying to you, NiNi," Addie said. "But we needed a detective to investigate Daddy's case."

Sebastian, still holding the stunned NiNi's hand, escorted her to a meticulously clean living room of forest greens and browns. He lovingly deposited her on the couch and climbed up next to her. "Why don't we just sit here and get to know each other a little better? I'll start. I have an ungodly amount of money, and I know how to use it. What say you let me take you to dinner and a movie. Maybe a little dancing. See where the night takes us."

Addie stepped in front of NiNi and snapped her fingers. "Hey, NiNi. You alive in there?"

"Why am I holding hands with a talking chimp?"

"Kismet," Sebastian said. "Fate. Serendipity. Call it what you will, but it feels wonderful, doesn't it?"

"We told you," Addie said. "Sebastian's a detective, and he's going to prove that Daddy's innocent."

"Good luck with that," NiNi said, carefully extricating her hand from Sebastian's. "But this is a joke, right? He's one of your little friends in a chimp costume." She gave Sebastian's ear a tug.

"Ow, be careful. I only have two of 'em."

NiNi inspected Sebastian's head with both hands, pinching his cheeks, tousling his hair—anything to confirm his authenticity. "You're a real chimp."

Sebastian savored her touch. "In the flesh."

"Sorry." NiNi patted his hair back into place. "Didn't mean to rough you up there, but this is feeling like a really weird dream."

"If it is, I never want to wake up."

"What's gotten into you, Monkey?" Addie said. "It's just NiNi."

"My apologies." Sebastian gave NiNi a courteous bow. "But you are a beautiful, beautiful woman. And I was led to believe you were their elderly grandmother."

NiNi was appalled. "How old did you say I was?"

"Don't look at me," Addie said. "I never even mentioned you're almost fifty."

"She says it like it's a death sentence," NiNi said. "But thank you for the lovely compliments, Sebastian. Nice to know someone still thinks I look good for my age."

"You look great for any age."

"Listen to you." NiNi blushed. "Such a flirt. And my name is Valerie, by the way."

"Valerie, Valerie, Valerie. A more lyrical poem has never been written."

"Quit being gross, Monkey," Addie said. "We've got a murder to solve."

"Are you really a detective?" NiNi asked.

"Yeah, Sebastian," Bennett said, "how *did* you become a detective?"

Sebastian bounded off the couch and gripped the lapels of his smoking jacket. "Gather 'round children, and I will regale you with the story of how I became the greatest detective in the world."

Addie and Bennett scooted to take positions on either side of their NiNi. Once settled in, the captivated audience hung on Sebastian's every word.

"It all started on a nature preserve in Fresno, California, just a baby chimp and a crazy dream. Never knew my real parents. Was abandoned in a wicker basket. Perhaps a traveling circus left me behind. Or maybe a movie production company no longer needed my services. Either way, my earliest memories are of my human father, John Winthrop. He was a caretaker at the nature preserve. A widower with no family of his own, he was an affable gentleman with a big push-broom mustache and an even bigger heart. He doted on me like a proud poppa."

"We saw his portrait at Sebastian's house," Bennett said to NiNi.

"Yeah, he's dead," Addie said, contributing the sad fact with brutal honesty.

"I'm so sorry," NiNi said. "My condolences."

Sebastian acknowledged the considerate comment with a sincere nod of gratitude and then continued his tale. "He loved watching old TV shows, and I fell asleep each night to the adventures of Columbo, Banacek, Mannix, and other detective geniuses. I suppose I learned to talk by watching so much TV. Father didn't tell anyone because he didn't want me whisked away to some research lab, so we just minded our own business, watched our shows, and lived a perfectly quiet, happy life. Then, one day, we read about the theft of the Moussajian Red Diamond, one of the most precious stones in the world, which at the time had an estimated value of twelve million dollars. The diamond was on a tour of the United States when it was purloined from a local museum. The company that had insured the diamond offered a significant reward for its safe return, and I knew it was the perfect opportunity for me to demonstrate my detective skills. I will save the details of the case for another time, but they do involve several foot chases, a memorable encounter with a motorcycle gang, and plenty of kung-fu. Needless to say, I found the diamond and collected the reward. That initial success led to other insurance companies hiring us, and we'd get anywhere from ten to fifteen percent of the value recovered. It was the same basic model that my hero Thomas Banacek, as portrayed by the legendary George Peppard, used on TV. Of course, Father acted as the frontman, and no one knew that a talking chimp was the true brains of the operation, but eventually we gave up the charade. You'd be surprised how little anyone cares you're a talking chimp when you're saving them millions of dollars."

"How come I never heard about you on the news?" NiNi said. "A talking chimp is a pretty big deal."

"There was a brief moment when I made national headlines, but the very same day my story broke, a famous Instagram influencer got a new hat."

"Yeah, that'll happen. How did you end up in Hadleyburg?"

"Father grew up here. I spent many a night listening to him spin yarns about his hometown and how nothing was more beautiful than the rolling hills of Southwestern Pennsylvania. When he died, I decided to retire here with my cat Sidney and see for myself."

"Oh, you have a cat?"

"He's dead too," Addie said.

"I'm so sorry. Do you at least like it here in Hadleyburg?"

"Not particularly, no." The years of sadness showed on Sebastian's face. However, his dour expression quickly brightened, and he gazed lovingly at NiNi. "But things are looking up."

She laughed. "You're a little devil. But do you really think my son-on-law is innocent?"

"You don't?"

Painfully aware of Addie and Bennett's hopes for their father's acquittal, she seemed to choose her words carefully. "I suppose…anything is possible."

"Does that mean we can count on your help in our investigation?"

"What do you mean *our* investigation?" NiNi said. "Isn't it *your* investigation?"

Addie climbed on her grandmother's lap. "C'mon, NiNi, Monkey needs all the help he can get. Look at him. He can barely dress himself."

"I just don't know if I want my grandchildren mixed up in a murder investigation."

"But he really does need us," Bennett said. "Right, Sebastian?"

"The children have been extremely helpful in identifying possible suspects and teaching me about the local wrestling scene. Things will go much smoother if they're around. Of course, if you're worried about keeping them out of trouble, you could always join us."

NiNi pondered the chimp's proposition while her grandchildren pleaded with her to say yes. The persistent pestering paid off.

"Okay, but we probably shouldn't tell your mother about this. There's no way she'd approve, and if she ever found out I was letting you hang out with a talking chimp, she'd probably never speak to me again."

"No worries, NiNi," Addie said. "We can keep a secret. Did you ever find out about that dent in your car?"

"What dent?"

"Exactly. What's our next move, Monkey?"

"Your next move," NiNi said, "is getting cleaned up before your mother gets here. We'll resume the investigation tomorrow. Sebastian, you can meet us here at nine."

"In the morning?" Sebastian said. "What am I, a farmer?"

"Their mother drops them off on her way to work, and then she picks them up at six o'clock. That's the window we have to get stuff done. Okay, you two, say goodbye to Sebastian and then go get ready for dinner."

Addie was first, giving him a quick wave and saying, "Peace out, Monkey. Try not to be so stupid tomorrow."

While his sister ran upstairs to wash up, Bennett gave Sebastian a hug. "Thanks for all your help, Sebastian. We really appreciate it."

The great chimp detective was visibly uncomfortable with the blatant show of affection but offered a clumsy pat on the back to send Bennett on his way. NiNi walked Sebastian to the door.

"They really are great kids," she said.

"One out of two ain't bad."

"Addie's been giving you a hard time, huh?"

"Little bit."

"She's a pistol. Everyone says she takes after me."

"Thanks for the warning."

"Do you really think their father is innocent?"

Sebastian stood tall, chest out. "I stake my professional reputation upon it."

"And if you can't trust the professional reputation of a talking chimp detective…. You better go home and get some sleep. I'll see you bright and early tomorrow morning."

"Looking forward to it," Sebastian said. "And I don't say that often."

He nodded farewell and descended the front porch steps toward Ol' Blue.

Before shutting the front door, NiNi called out, "And, hey, don't listen to Addie. I like the way you dress."

"Oh yeah?"

"You look very handsome."

Sebastian winked at her. "And don't you forget it."

CHAPTER THIRTEEN

Sebastian arrived at NiNi's house precisely at 9:00 a.m. He actually got there fifteen minutes early, but he sat in Ol' Blue and watched the dashboard clock, nervously adjusting his ascot and smoothing his hair, until the time was right. He ascended the porch steps with his usual elegance before placing a firm, rhythmic knock on the front door. Addie welcomed him.

"Again with the smoking jacket?"

"Every detective needs a signature look. Columbo had his raincoat. Banacek had his turtlenecks. I have my smoking jacket, ascot, and stylish khakis. Learn to appreciate it."

"Hey, Sebastian," Bennett said, running to join his sister at the front door. "What's the plan for today?"

"I managed to secure a ten a.m. interview with Jill Johnson to get the dirt on why she was prescribing Mitch those pain medications. After that, we'll check in on Vince Manero, and then we'll finish up with Lenny Lambda and the Hickson Brothers. From what Thacker told us, they seemed to have a pretty intense professional rivalry with Mitch. Where there's emotion, there could be motive. And speaking of emotion, where is that lovely NiNi of yours?"

"Right here." NiNi floated down the stairs like a dream, her chestnut locks bouncing on the shoulders of a crisp linen blouse. "And I'm driving. Addie told me about your choice in music."

"Fine with me," Sebastian said. "Someone of my social stature really should have a chauffeur."

"What's a *show-fer?*" Addie asked.

"It's a French word that means driver," NiNi said.

Addie hitched her thumb at Sebastian. "Should have known Mr. Fancy Pants here can't just talk normal good English like us."

"Yes," Sebastian said, "it's a real shame."

"Also heard that you call your car Ol' Blue," NiNi said.

"A name fit for a king."

"I named mine after the world's greatest detective."

"How could you possibly have named your car after me when we just met?"

"Don't be stupid, Monkey," Addie said. "It's the Batmobile."

Sebastian seemed confused. "You named your car after a winged rodent?"

"Batman is the best detective ever," NiNi said.

"Batman's not real, I am. And if we're considering fictional detectives, Columbo would detect circles around that bat-brained doofus."

"Don't be jealous."

"Why would I be jealous of someone who wears a stupid outfit, hangs out in a cave all day, and works with children?"

Addie laughed. "You wear that dopey smoking jacket, your house is basically a cave, and you're working with us. Now who's the bat-brained doofus?" She dropped an imaginary microphone.

Sebastian lowered his head in shame. "What has become of me?"

NiNi's Batmobile, a matte black SUV, was a definite step up from Ol' Blue, as it had a touch-screen console, power windows, a working air conditioner, and all the other basic amenities found in motor vehicles manufactured within the past thirty-five years. While Sebastian was allowed to ride up front, Addie insisted on controlling the musical selection, and she chose some sort of techno dance nonsense that had Sebastian questioning his sanity. Thankfully, the drive to Happy Smile Dental Associates, where Dr. Jill Johnson plied her craft, was mercifully short. And when NiNi pulled into the parking lot, Sebastian suggested a slight alteration to the morning's itinerary.

"You know what? There's no need for all four of us to go traipsing into Jill's office to interview her. Addie and I will handle this. And I am feeling a might peckish. Why don't you and Bennett go to that coffee shop across the street there and get us some snacks. My treat."

NiNi stopped Sebastian from reaching for his wallet. "That's okay, I got it. What did you want?"

"Maybe just a sparkling water and—"

"Cake pops!" Addie yelled.

"What's a cake pop?"

"They're like cake, but in a pop shape."

"Pop isn't a shape."

"They're basically donut holes on a stick," Bennett said.

"They're air on a stick?"

"Forget it, Monkey," Addie said. "NiNi, get cake pops. Lots of 'em."

"What flavors?"

"Surprise us. C'mon, Monkey, we got a suspect to question."

Happy Smile Dental Associates had three dentists on staff, but only one of them had a potential connection to Mitch Mayhem's murder. Sebastian opened the door for Addie, and they entered a long, skinny waiting room with eight chairs on the left and a sign-in window and a glass door on the right. A TV mounted in the room's far corner displayed some insipid morning show, but the hosts' mindless banter was still insufficient to drown out the whirring machines and whooshing spit vacuums.

"Go ahead and sit down," Sebastian said. "I'll let them know we're here."

Addie walked past the doomed—a frail middle-aged gentleman with a slightly puffy cheek and nervousness in his eyes, a young woman with a jittery leg, and an elderly nun counting rosary beads— and sat in the very last chair. A few seconds later, Sebastian joined her, the presence of a talking chimp in a smoking jacket not registering with those awaiting the drill.

Sebastian selected a magazine from the end table next to his chair. "Might be a minute. Want something to read?"

"No thanks." Addie leaned closer to Sebastian and whispered, "Get a load of those saps. I wouldn't trade places with them for anything."

"Dentists aren't so bad."

"Are you nuts? They're the worst. Who grows up wanting to put their fingers in other people's mouths? Mommy and Daddy were making me go every six months for a while there, but I think they forgot, because I haven't had an appointment since the start of last school year. And don't you go reminding them."

Sebastian half-heartedly flipped through the pages of his magazine. "Things been busy at home?"

"Between you and me, Mommy and Daddy haven't really been getting along lately. Don't tell Bennett."

"Sorry to hear it. Have they been arguing a lot?"

"Kind of." She took Sebastian's magazine and studied the cover, which featured surgically enhanced celebrities with disingenuous grins. "But usually when they fight, they just get real quiet and don't talk to each other much. And Mommy's so busy with work and school, she hasn't been much fun lately."

The door next to the sign-in window opened, and a young woman in blue OR scrubs said, "Sister Seton?" The elderly nun stood with the assistance of a cane and was helped into the back.

Addie elbowed Sebastian. "Lot of good all that praying did her. I'm so glad we're just here to talk to Jill."

"Yeah, that's what we're here for all right. Just going to talk to Jill. Nothing else. What's your mom going to school for?"

"Some stupid law stuff. Nothing cool. She's a secretary at a law firm, and if she graduates, she can help them in court or something. She's getting one of the lawyers there to take Daddy's case."

"They any good?"

"Doubt it. They don't even have commercials on TV. If I ever need a lawyer, I'm hiring Chester R. Snyder," she lowered her voice and pointed at Sebastian, mimicking the famous attorney's popular commercial, "because he gets money for you."

"I don't think he handles murder cases though."

"Didn't say I was gonna murder someone."

Sebastian saw the young woman in OR scrubs making her way to the glass door to announce the next patient. "Promise you'll never murder someone?"

Addie crossed her heart. "Promise."

"Remember you said that."

The young woman opened the door. "Addie?"

Sebastian raised his hand. "Here she is." He stood up, but Addie snagged him by the smoking jacket.

"Why did she call my name?"

"Because Jill's ready to be interviewed."

"Then why didn't she say *your* name too?"

"She did."

"No she didn't."

"You sure? Could have sworn she did."

"You made an appointment for me."

"What? Don't be ridiculous."

Addie dropped her magazine and latched onto the chair's armrests. "I'm not going anywhere."

"C'mon, we can't keep her waiting." Sebastian tried to pull Addie along with him, but she wriggled free and belly flopped on the seat of the chair, clutching it for dear life. He dragged her and the chair a few feet before realizing the futility of the situation. He turned to the dental hygienist and smiled. "One moment please."

Sebastian crouched next to Addie. "The only way I could get us in was to make an appointment. You either spend a few minutes in a dentist's chair, or your father spends the rest of his life in prison. Your call."

Addie, the side of her face still plastered against the seat cushion, squinted at her tormentor. "I'm gonna get you, Monkey. If it's the last thing I ever do, I'm gonna get you."

"Always good to have dreams. Now, up you go."

Addie peeled herself from the chair and tried to recapture some sense of decorum. She held her head high and marched toward the hygienist like a defiant soldier facing a firing squad.

"Sorry," Sebastian said to the hygienist. "She gets a little nervous."

"Don't worry about it. Happens all the time." She held the door for Sebastian. "Excuse me, but…are you a monkey?"

"No," Sebastian said, "but thanks for asking."

The hygienist led them down a hall to a small office on the left. She got Addie situated in the dental chair and then exited, saying that Dr. Johnson would join them momentarily. Addie folded her arms and sulked, her mouth pulled tighter than a balloon knot.

"You mad?"

Addie stared straight ahead, refusing to acknowledge him.

"She won't even have a chance to look at your teeth." He took a seat on a rolling stool next to the chair and started poking around the various dental tools. "As soon as she gets in here, we'll start asking her questions, and before you know it, it'll be time to leave."

Addie shot him a sideways glare.

"You've got nothing to worry about." Sebastian selected one of the tooth clearers attached to a hose and squirted some water into his mouth. Refreshed, he offered it to Addie. "Want some?"

"You shouldn't be touching that."

"Who are you, the dental police?" He took another drink. "Hey, watch this." He held the nozzle at arm's length and shot the water into the air like a fountain. The stream soared over his head, sprinkling the white cabinet doors and countertop, until he made the necessary adjustments to maneuver it into his mouth.

"Quit it," Addie said. "You're gonna get us in trouble."

Sebastian wiped water from his face. "You look like you need to cool off."

"Don't you dare."

The warning went unheeded, and a short burst of water struck her in the chest. Shocked, Addie looked down at the stain on her shirt. "I can't believe you—" Another volley landed, this time catching her in the face. She dove at Sebastian. "Gimme that thing!"

The two combatants wrestled for the tooth cleaner even as the water continued to spray. Addie stood up in the dental chair to gain leverage, and whatever water didn't find the ceiling and walls ended up on her—the wet streaks across her shirt and jeans making it look like she had run through a carwash. But her persistence paid off, and she eventually yanked the tooth cleaner from Sebastian and silenced the stream. She took a moment to revel in her success, standing with one foot on the dental chair's armrest like a victorious gladiator, before aiming the nozzle at her defeated foe. "Dance, Monkey."

The office door swung open. Dr. Jill Johnson stopped dead when she saw the soaked Addie about to open fire. Addie sheepishly lowered her weapon, and a grateful Sebastian greeted his savior.

"Dr. Johnson, I presume." She was just as pretty in person as she was in the photos they had found in Mitch's basement, although her silky auburn hair was a bit longer now and fell well past the shoulders of her lab coat. Her delicate features made her seem far more like a ballerina than a weekend wrestler. "I'm Sebastian, Addie's uncle. I told her not to touch that thing, but you know kids. Anyway, Addie was telling me all about you on the way over here. A pleasure to meet you."

A confused Jill shook Sebastian's hand. "You're her uncle?"

"Yes, on her mother's side. You can probably see the resemblance. But I'm helping out around the house while her father is away."

"Of course." Jill helped Addie sit back down in the dentist chair and then returned the tooth cleaner to its stand.

"I'm sorry," Addie said. "I didn't mean to—"

"Shhh." Jill pulled Addie in for a hug. "You poor, poor girl. I was so surprised when I saw your name on my patient list. I thought your dad said you guys went to Dr. Bernthal? But that doesn't matter. You're here now. How have you been doing, honey?"

With her face smooshed against the bosom of Jill's white dental smock, Addie managed a garbled, "Okay."

Jill gave Addie a final squeeze and then held her at arm's length so she could make deliberate eye contact. "I just want you to know that I don't think your father did it. And if there's anything you or your brother need, I'm here for you."

"Oh, don't worry about that," Sebastian said. "Her Uncle Sebastian is taking real good care of her, isn't that right, Addie? Of course it is. But, Dr. Johnson, I'm relieved to hear that you share our view of her father's innocence."

"I've known Stanley for years, and he doesn't have a mean bone in his body. Sure, he plays a heel in the ring, but he's a sweetheart. He'd never hurt anyone."

"But if Daddy didn't do it," Addie said, "and we all know he didn't, then who did?"

"That's really a matter for the police, sweetie. I wouldn't know where to begin. I mean, we're hardly detectives."

Addie pointed at Sebastian. "He is."

"You're a detective?"

"Yes, the truth is I am not Addie's uncle. Although, deep down, you probably already knew that just because of how handsome I am and my enviable fashion sense. But I am one of the world's great detectives. Why am I being so humble? I'm the greatest. Addie and her brother hired me to prove their father's innocence, and that investigation has led us here today."

"You don't think I did it, do you?"

"No one's saying that. But…jealousy can be a powerful motive for murder."

"Why would I be jealous of Mitch?"

"Weren't you two dating?"

"That was years ago."

"I see. You wanted to get back together, he wasn't interested, so you—"

"Are you crazy? I broke up with him. Believe me, that was one of the best decisions I ever made."

"Why's that?"

"Mitch wasn't exactly a good boyfriend. He cheated on me. A lot."

"Oh, I gotcha," Addie said, nodding. "Like when Mommy makes up words in Scrabble."

"Not exactly. You know how your mommy and daddy like to hug and kiss each other?"

Addie shook her head.

"Really?"

"I've seen Mommy cheat on Scrabble way more."

"That's sad. Well, most mommies and daddies like to do that sort of stuff, but Mitch liked to be daddy with lots of different mommies. Sometimes two or three at a time."

"I think we get the picture," Sebastian said.

"Seriously, you wouldn't believe how many."

"We don't really need—"

"Or how cheap and trashy these mommies were."

"Okay, forget all that. Was he seeing anyone before his death?"

"Not that I know of. He had actually been pretty bitter and standoffish the last few months. Wasn't going out much. He just did the shows and went straight home."

"Maybe he was injured or in pain."

"Didn't show it in the ring."

"Then why were you prescribing him pain medication?"

"You know about that?"

"Was he a patient?"

"Not exactly. Please don't tell anyone. I swear, I only ever did it for him. No one else."

"But why'd you do it at all?"

Jill glanced at Addie and seemed to choose her words carefully. "Let's just say Mitch had some home movies of us being a mommy and daddy. And they were a little embarrassing."

"Like birthday parties and stuff?" Addie said. "I hate when mom gets videos of me wearing those stupid hats."

"If the videos were ever made public, they might harm my reputation as a doctor."

"He was blackmailing you?" Sebastian said.

"Pretty much, yeah."

"That's a real strong motive for murder."

"But I didn't do it. You believe me, don't you, Addie?"

"I wanna believe you, Jill. I mean, you're really nice. I like your hair and how it's always so shiny. And you love wrestling. Those are all good things. But, you are a dentist, so…."

"You know who probably did it? Lenny Lambda. You want to talk about jealousy, Lenny was definitely jealous of Mitch. When Mitch came back to the company last year, he took the top spot, and Lenny thought he should have been on top. And they did not get along."

"Why not?" Sebastian asked.

"Just different wrestling philosophies. They butted heads a lot. As a veteran, Mitch tried to help Lenny along and give him some advice, but Lenny just blew him off."

"We've been hearing similar stories from others. Was Mitch really that difficult to work with?"

"He had strong beliefs about what wrestling should be. If he liked you and thought you respected the business, there wasn't anything he wouldn't do for you. Super loyal. But if you crossed him, he just cut you off cold. No coming back from that. He was done with you."

"From what we hear, seems like Vince Manero and Mad Mike Dean also had problems with Mitch."

"It would be easier to say who didn't have a problem with him. But at least Manero and Dean are veterans who've been around a long time, so Mitch respected them. He did not respect Lenny, at all."

"Did Mitch respect Tony Katsaros?"

Jill laughed. "Of course not. But Tony idolized Mitch, so he let him do whatever he wanted."

"Sounds like you don't respect Tony much either."

"You're not going to get me to say anything bad about Tony. After all, I am his women's champion. But most of the guys just see him as a money mark. As long as he keeps paying, they'll keep being his friends."

"You know, I think he has a crush on you."

"Have you been reading the dirt sheets? Anytime a woman has success in this business, rumors always start that she's—playing mommy and daddy with the promotor. Don't get me wrong, Tony's a sweet kid and all—"

"Kid?" Addie said. "Isn't he like forty?"

"Yeah, you know what? I think he is. Funny, he just always seems so much younger than that. But I swear, there's nothing going on between us."

"Can you think of anyone else who could have done it?" Sebastian asked.

"Again, that's a pretty long list. But I'd focus on Lenny if I were you. The most important thing is that I didn't do it. I cannot stress that enough."

"I tend to believe you."

"Really?"

"Whoever killed Mitch also stole his championship title. You're the women's champ, so why would you care about the men's title?"

"That's right. I wouldn't, and I don't. Excellent point."

"The killer also has to be very strong, and I doubt you have the physical strength necessary to have committed the crime."

Jill wrinkled her brow. "You don't think I'm strong?"

"It's not that, it's just you're not very big, and—"

"Oh, it's because I'm a woman, is that it?" She stood and sent the stool crashing into the cabinet behind her. "You wanna go?"

Sebastian begged off. While Addie no doubt would have loved seeing Jill stretch the chimp like taffy, she said, "Jill, he thinks you're innocent. Don't make him change his mind."

"You're right. Sorry about that. You know what they say: You can take the girl out of the wrestling ring, but…she'll still beat you senseless if you say something stupid. I'm just glad you guys know I'm innocent. I mean, Addie, you trust me, right?"

"Sure."

"Good, because when you were talking earlier, I think I saw a little something." Jill trapped Addie's jaw and asked her to open wide. "Uh oh. Looks like Mr. Tooth Decay paid a visit. But we caught it early. Just a quick little filling and you'll be good to go. And it's on the house. No charge."

Addie looked to Sebastian for help.

"That's very kind of you, Dr. Johnson," Sebastian said. "I know Addie appreciates you taking such good care of her."

"It's the least I can do." Jill activated the hydraulics in the chair, and Addie began lowering backward into a reclined position.

She clutched at Sebastian's smoking jacket. "Monkey, don't I have to—"

"Take better care of your teeth? Probably." He pulled free of her. "I'll be out in the car if you need me. Thanks again, Dr. Johnson."

The last thing Sebastian heard before closing the office door was the metallic hum of a dentist's drill. He found NiNi and Bennett waiting for him in the parking lot. They were parked a few spots to the left of the front door and were sampling their recent purchases, with NiNi sipping a tall coffee and Bennett nibbling a bran muffin. After informing them of Addie's dental procedure, Sebastian filled them in on the conversation with Jill, noting that Mitch Mayhem was indeed a creep and that Lenny Lambda was now their prime suspect. He spent the remainder of the wait enjoying some sparking mineral water and banana bread cake pops.

It was a good twenty minutes before Jill walked an angry Addie to the front door of the Happy Smile Dental Associates, unleashing her like a tiny tornado on an unsuspecting trailer park. Addie failed to return NiNi's wave but simply stomped to the rear passenger door with vengeance in her eyes and malice in her heart. She climbed into the back seat next to Bennett and slammed the door shut. All eyes turned to her in fear of the inevitable eruption, but she hunkered down in her seat, silently fuming like the smokestack of an overworked steel mill. Her right cheek and lower lip showed a slight droop, indicating the recent Novocain injection.

"How'd it go?" NiNi asked, observing her granddaughter in the rearview mirror.

"You look great," Sebastian said. "No one will even notice that little drooling thing you have going on there."

"Mumpy," Addie said through numb lips, "I'b gonna kilb youb."

She launched herself at Sebastian, but Bennett managed to block the assault, stopping her from perpetrating child-on-chimp violence.

"Addelynn Marie, you settle your tea kettle right now!" NiNi said. "Sebastian is doing all this to save your father from prison, and he apparently cares more about your dental hygiene than you do, so you should be glad that you're walking around with one less cavity in your head."

"Bub, MiMi—"

"Don't 'but, NiNi' me. Apologize to Sebastian."

Addie fell back into her seat and folded her arms, her droopy lip enhancing her petulant pout. "I'b sorry, Sebashban."

"Duly noted."

NiNi said, "And?"

"Remember to brush twice a day and floss between meals."

"Isn't there something else you would like to say to Addie?"

"Can't think of anything."

"Sebastian."

The chimp detective sighed. "Addie, I'm sorry I tricked you into seeing a dentist."

Addie looked to Bennett in shocked surprise. Upon confirming that she had actually heard Sebastian apologize, she beamed with profound satisfaction and said, "Aboloby accebbed."

"Great, here." Sebastian handed her a cake pop covered in white icing and rainbow sprinkles. "Get started on your next cavity."

Addie's eyes lit up. She bit into the tasty treat, and her head bobbed in happiness, even as the crumbs tumbled from her numb mouth.

CHAPTER FOURTEEN

Next on the agenda was paying a visit to Vince Manero, the aging rockstar wannabe who Mitch Mayhem refused to work with. Manero ran Pinnacle Motors, a used car lot that had fewer vehicles than Sebastian's garage. The selection was mostly mid-sized sedans and nondescript compact cars.

"Remember," Sebastian said to NiNi as she parked the Batmobile in front of the lot's small office building, "let me do all the talking. Murder investigations are delicate matters. I've already been teaching Addie and Bennett the finer points of being a detective, so just follow my lead."

"Got it," NiNi said.

The four detectives exited the Batmobile, Addie still trying to poke feeling into her numb lower lip. Before they could even shut their doors, Manero slithered from the small office building with a fake smile plastered on his overly spray-tanned face. He was short and thickly built, the loose flesh of advancing age making him resemble an old bulldog stuffed into a Hawaiian shirt and strained khakis. The shirt was left unbuttoned to showcase a tangle of gold chains atop a sunken chest. He zeroed in on NiNi, his long mane of dirty blond hair swaying like dried straw.

"She sure is a beauty," he said as way of welcome. "The car's not bad either." He paired the comment with a wink that would make a skeleton's skin crawl. "Lookin' to sell?"

Sebastian sauntered over with his usual dignified air. "Good afternoon, my good man. My associates and I represent—"

"Where were you when Mitch Mayhem got murdered?" NiNi said.

"What?"

NiNi slammed her car door. "You heard me."

"Byah," the numb-lipped Addie said, rushing to her grandmother's side. "You hearbb her."

Manero backed up. "Whoa, what's this about?"

Sebastian jumped between the opposing parties and smiled at Manero. "Could you give us a moment please?" He held his cheery demeanor until Manero drifted away, and then he turned to NiNi in dismay. "What was that?"

"Thought we'd do like a good cop/bad cop thing."

"You can't just rush into something like that. Good cop/bad cop requires extensive preparation and meticulous planning. Who's the good cop? What's our motivation? What leverage can we use? These things have to be discussed."

"I'm the bad cop, you're the good cop. There, we've discussed it." NiNi brushed past him, Addie in tow. Sebastian looked to Bennett for help.

The junior detective said, "NiNi's gonna NiNi."

And she was in the process of doing just that, advancing once more on their suspect. "Hey, hotshot, you still haven't answered the question."

"They caught the guy who killed Mitch."

"Babby bibn't boo it!" Addie said.

"She drunk?"

"She's Bonecrusher's kid," NiNi said. "I'm his mother-in-law, and we know he didn't do it. So, why don't you tell us who did before we have to get rough."

"I like the sound of that. How about we talk this out over some drinks at my place? I'm sure we'd be able to get to the bottom of things."

"Uh, hello," Sebastian said, waving his arms. "I'm right here."

Manero looked over at the neglected chimp. "What?"

"We arrived together. Why would you assume we're not a couple?"

"But we're not a couple," NiNi said.

"We could be. Sure, there are clearly some obstacles in the way, like you being the grandmother of one child and one hellspawn and me being from a much higher social stratus, but I'd be willing to overlook those flaws. Regardless, that's not the point. He doesn't know our situation. And I consider his behavior shockingly disrespectful."

"Sorry, little buddy," Manero said. "I just thought she's a smokin' hot lady, and you're a, you know…monkey."

"That's speciesism, discrimination based on one's species. And I will not tolerate it."

"Hey now, that's not fair. Some of my best friends are monkeys. I go to the zoo like twice a year."

"You're making it worse."

"Listen, didn't mean to upset you. Let me make it right. I'll answer whatever questions you want. I've got nothing to hide."

"Start with where you were on the night Mitch died," NiNi said.

"I went out after the show. Ran into some groupies. Had a real good time. Didn't get home until the next morning, if you catch my meaning. And I know that you do."

"So help me, if you wink at me one more time, I'll—" NiNi sniffed the air and looked around. "Is someone burning moldy tires?"

"That's my cologne," Manero said. "Only available at finer Guatemalan gas stations. Drives the girls wild. But I guess you already know that, huh?"

Sensing that NiNi the bad cop was about to get violent, Sebastian changed the subject. "How long did you know Mitch?"

"We went way back." Manero sucked in his stomach and tried to look less bloated. "You may not be able to tell by looking at me, but I've been wrestling for over thirty years."

"Is that all?" NiNi said.

"The reason I've been able to have such a long career is that I constantly reinvent myself. Right now, I'm living this rockstar gimmick. It's just me turned up to eleven. Because I really am a lead singer for a hard rock band called *Kermit*. You probably heard of us." He ignored the blank stares to the contrary and continued. "When I come to the ring, the crowd always sings one of my songs. That never happened in all of wrestling until I came along."

"Bit's bo bupid," Addie said.

"What did she say?"

"She loves it," Bennett said, offering a much kinder translation.

"You're not alone, little girl," Manero said. "Everybody does. But I'll probably change it up soon. Who knows? Maybe tomorrow I'll wake up and want to be a wizard. I could make it work. Would you like to see me be a wizard, little girl?"

"Bo, bo bupid."

"Of course you would. I was already on top when Mitch was breaking in. Took him under my wing. Showed him the ropes. Without me, there never would have been a Mitch Mayhem."

"Then why was he so mad at you?" Sebastian said.

"Who says he was mad?"

"The only reason his last match was against Bonecrusher was because he refused to work with you."

"Shouldn't believe what you read in the dirt sheets."

"We got it from Tony Katsaros himself."

"You talked to Tony? You're really digging into this thing, aren't ya?"

"Be're bebectives," Addie said, her chin held high.

Manero lifted his hand in front of his mouth and whispered to NiNi and Sebastian, "Seriously, you might want to look into a speech therapist or something. Can't understand a thing she says. All pops and buzzes."

"Word on the street is you were feeding fake news to Steve Thacker to make Mitch look bad," Sebastian said. "I even heard that he called you a stooge in his final promo."

"Mitch thought everyone was out to get him. Why would I need to plant stories? He never missed a chance to make himself look bad."

"But you couldn't have been happy about losing your main-event spot," NiNi said. "And as long as Mitch was holding the title, you'd never get another shot at being champion. That ate you up inside, didn't it?"

"You're cute when you're angry."

"Never being champion again. Never feeling that respect and adulation from the fans. Made you feel old. Weak. Less of a man. You couldn't take it, could you?"

Manero laughed.

"There was only one solution, one way for you to get what you wanted, to recapture that former glory of your youth. Mitch had to go. So, you killed him."

"You're nuts. But lucky for you, I have a thing for crazy chicks." Manero slipped his arm around NiNi. "How about we ditch the monkey and the two brats and finish our little discussion in priv—hey!"

NiNi snared Manero's wrist and judo flipped him to the asphalt. "Don't ever touch me. C'mon, guys," she said, directing Addie, Bennett, and Sebastian toward the Batmobile. "I think we're done here."

Sebastian noticed that Manero's cell phone had fallen from his pocket. He reached down to retrieve it and saw a missed call from Steve Thacker. Sebastian filed away that interesting bit of information and returned the phone to the dazed Manero, who was still laid out like a beached walrus.

"And in case you're wondering, she was the bad cop."

CHAPTER FIFTEEN

Back on the road again, Sebastian informed the others of Manero's missed call.

"Likely proves that he was Thacker's source for those negative stories about Mitch," Sebastian said. "But that's not nearly as surprising as your judo skills. Where did you learn to do that?"

"Competed growing up," NiNi said.

"She won trophies," Bennett added from the back seat, the pride for his grandmother evident in his voice.

"I can see why," Sebastian said. "But I hope you know that I was about to intervene."

NiNi consulted her driver's side mirror and changed lanes. "Uh-huh."

"No, really. I was about to twist that creep into a pretzel."

"Oh, I believe you."

"He got off easy if you ask me."

"No doubt."

"I'm not kidding."

"Why would you be? So, where to?"

Sebastian side-eyed her with skepticism. "The Bullseye store. Lenny Lambda and the Hickson Brothers work there."

"And they're the ones who got in the fight in the dressing room with Mitch the night he died, right?"

"Yeah," Addie said, still massaging the feeling back into her face. "It wab bo fummy. MiMi, you coulb have beatem all ub."

Sebastian spun in his seat to look back at Addie. "What about me?"

"MiMi coulb beat you ub too."

"That's not what I meant."

"My bab. Whub you meam?"

"If I could have beaten them up."

Addie laughed and laughed and laughed.

* * *

Hadleyburg, Pennsylvania, was once famous for having not one but *two* covered shopping malls. Today, one of those malls was a distant memory, replaced by a sprawling assortment of restaurants and discount stores, while the other continued to stagger toward bankruptcy, pinning its hopes on a recently opened casino that promised a glimmer of excitement in an otherwise dull existence. Most citizens who still opted to do their shopping in person did so at either the Bullseye or the All-Mart, and the two big-box behemoths stood on opposite sides of the same intersection, heightening the somewhat one-sided rivalry. While it was running a clear second, the Bullseye anchored a plaza with a Giant Eagle grocery store, a Lowe's home improvement, and a few chain restaurants, creating what passed for Hadleyburg's cultural district.

The Bullseye wasn't very crowded for a Tuesday afternoon, and NiNi managed to get a spot not far from the entrance. The great chimp detective and his three apprentices exited the Batmobile determined to uncover something—anything—that could solve Mitch Mayhem's murder.

Sebastian tightened his smoking jacket. "Remember, I'm in charge here. Got it?"

"Sure," NiNi said. She gave Bennett a sly wink.

"I should really handle Lenny," Addie said. "I know I could break that little punk. Give me two minutes alone with him, and—" She wiggled her mouth like a bunny with an itchy nose. "I can feel my lips again."

"Our long national nightmare is over," Sebastian said.

"Don't get smart, Monkey. But, hey, while we're here, you should get some jeans."

"I don't wear *jeans*." He spoke the last word as if it were caked in sewage.

"Yeah, I know. That's the problem."

"I hardly think being fashionable is a problem."

"Jeans are way cooler than those old man pants you got on."

"Says you."

"Normal people wear jeans."

"Who wants to be normal?"

"I think you'd look pretty cute in jeans," NiNi said.

Sebastian stopped in his tracks. "Is that right?"

Just then, a loud crash sounded in the parking lot behind them, followed by fits of buffoonish laughter. Sebastian and his companions saw two Bullseye employees—recognizable by their distinctive blue shirts—sitting on the asphalt with a pair of toppled shopping carts between them. The two men scampered to their feet, collected their respective carts, and took off running in opposite directions.

"Isn't that the Hickson Brothers?" Bennett said.

Closer inspection revealed that the two guffawing goofs were indeed the KCW Tag Team Champions. The great chimp detective and his associates watched as the two brothers reset their shopping carts, stared each other down, and then raced forward in a dead sprint, the shopping cart wheels a steady rumble beneath their moronic battle cries. The plastic carts slammed into each other, and the force of the bone-jarring collision sent both combatants tumbling to the pavement amidst more idiotic laughter.

The mindless hilarity didn't end until Ronnie Hickson glimpsed the approaching detectives and jumped up, a dim-witted smirk of superiority upon his smug face. "What are you looking at?"

Addie squared up to him, her fists at the ready. "A couple dummies."

Ricky Hickson, still brushing bits of gravel from his uniform pants, stumbled to his brother's side. "Aren't you Crusher's kids?"

"Yeah, we're Crusher's kids," Addie said. "That's our NiNi. And this right here is the best detective in the world," she swatted

Sebastian, "and he's gonna prove that you two dumb-dumbs croaked Mitch Mayhem."

Sebastian rubbed his arm where Addie had hit him. "That might be a bit aggressive. I mean, I am the best detective in the world, so that part's true. However, I have no reason to believe that you two murdered Mitch. But we would certainly appreciate your help in determining the real killer."

"Whoa," Ricky Hickson said. "It's a talkin' chipmunk."

"We saw the fight you had with him the night he died," Addie said. "That makes you prime suspects."

"Hold on," Sebastian said. "Did you just call me a chipmunk? Monkey I can understand. But chipmunk?"

Ricky Hickson pulled his brother back a bit. "Careful, bro. He might have rabies."

"If you'll just answer a few questions for us," NiNi said, "I'm sure we'll be able to get this whole mess cleared up."

"Hey, we don't have to talk to you, lady," Ronnie Hickson said. "We don't have to do anything. Unless Lenny tells us to."

"Why is no one else offended by this?" Sebastion said. "Chipmunks are filthy little rodents. Do I look like a filthy little rodent?"

Ricky Hickson paused. "Kind of."

"How dare you."

"Maybe we should just talk to Lenny," NiNi said.

Ronnie Hickson puffed out his underdeveloped chest. "Yeah, maybe you should."

He swung one of his stubby arms, motioning for them to follow. Ricky Hickson loped after his brother with oafish enthusiasm.

Incredulous, Sebastian looked up at NiNi and said, "I'm not a chipmunk."

She stroked his head. "It's okay. We know you're not a chipmunk."

"Yeah," Addie said. "Chipmunks are cute."

The Hickson Brothers led them through the parking lot to the main entrance. The store's signature bright blue façade accentuated the concentric yellow and red circles that constituted the company logo, creating an eye-catching presentation that no doubt lured eager shoppers. Unfortunately, the store's name, spelled out in large white letters mounted above the entrance, was short one L and a Y, welcoming customers to their neighborhood BUL SE E.

"Your sign's broken," Addie said.

"*Your* sign's broken," Ronnie Hickson said. The two dimwitted brothers high-fived each other.

The automatic sliding doors parted with a spastic lurch and sputtered to a halt after creating barely enough room for access. Ronnie Hickson wedged himself into the opening and strained to force the doors open until his brother provided assistance. The combined might of the two bumbling buffoons was enough to gain entry, and they tumbled free, each shoving the other and taking credit.

NiNi stepped between the doors and guarded against any further mechanical malfunctions, allowing Addie, Bennett, and Sebastian to pass through safely. "No wonder I never shop here."

Sebastian said, "I don't shop here because it's beneath me."

The faulty doors were a fitting welcome. The store's shabby tile flooring, marred with dirty footprints, gum wrappers, and any number of slip-and-fall hazards, failed to reflect the flickering fluorescent lighting. To the left, banks of empty registers sat unattended, silently mocking the line of customers patiently waiting for a lone cashier to figure out why a jumbo pack of toilet paper wouldn't scan. To the right, a snack bar employee whipped a towel at an overcooked hotdog, its charred remains flaming within the glass-enclosed broiler, and a jammed fountain drink dispenser poured an endless stream of Dr. Pepper into an overflowing cup. The smell of the burning processed tubular meat mingled with the scent of bleach-soaked pine cones, indicating that something must have been cleaned at some point, even though there was no visual evidence to support the claim. They advanced past a discount section of cardboard bins brimming with low-budget DVDs and six-month-old chocolate Santas to see the Hickson Brothers in the store's main thoroughfare, searching the chaotic mess of disorganized shelves and plundered clothing racks for any sign of their beloved leader.

"Go find Lenny," Ronnie Hickson said to his brother. "I'll stay here and make sure they don't cause any trouble." Ricky Hickson embarked on his mission with fervor, rushing off like a particularly puerile toddler.

Sebastian, repulsed that the soles of his handmade Italian loafers were sticking to the neglected floor tiles, said, "Yes, if left unattended, we might do something foolish like mop the floors."

"We lost our mop," Ronnie Hickson said.

"But you sell mops."

"Yeah," he pointed to the far corner of the store, "back there."

"Did you ever think of using one of those?"

"Just wait until Lenny gets here. Then we'll see what's up."

Addie stepped in front of Ronnie Hickson. "I'll tell you what's up. You shouldn't be tag team champs."

"Who says?"

"Me."

NiNi said, "Addie, you shouldn't—"

"No, NiNi, he needs to hear this."

Sebastian looked to NiNi. "See what I've been dealing with?"

"We're the best tag team in the world," Ronnie Hickson said. "Maybe you should read the Squared Circle sometime. Might learn something."

"You can't even wrestle."

"Yeah, okay. You know how stupid you sound right now?"

"News flash, dummy. Your little flippy gymnastics routines aren't wrestling. It's supposed to be a fight, not some goofy dance number."

"You don't know what you're talking about. We're revolutionizing the business."

"If that means killing it, then sure. And you're teeny-weeny. You and your dopey brother could never beat someone up. Heck, I bet me and my dopey brother could whoop you."

"Is that right?"

"Yeah, that's right."

"Prove it."

Addie pulled back her fist. "My pleasure—"

NiNi hooked Addie around the waist and yanked her backward, causing the wild haymaker to fall several feet short of its intended target. Ronnie Hickson cringed all the same.

"Okay, that's enough," NiNi said. She hoisted a still punching Addie into the air and started carrying her away. "Why don't we go do some shopping and let the boys handle this."

Addie struggled against her grandmother's grasp and yelled, "Drop the belts already!"

"We'll meet you guys back at the car," NiNi said. "And keep an eye on him for me."

Sebastian acknowledged the request with a wave. "Bennett is safe with me."

"I was talking to Bennett."

Even when NiNi and her hostage turned into the home appliance section, Addie could still be heard above the annoying in-store music, shouting vindictive threats that included such phrases as "stomp a mudhole in him" and "that stack of dimes he calls a neck."

Ronnie Hickson stood tall, or at least as tall as he could, and said, "Lucky she left when she did."

"That's funny," Sebastian said, "I'm usually the lucky one whenever she leaves. But now that it's just us fellas here, shoot me straight. Who had it in for Mitch Mayhem?"

"Who didn't? Nobody liked him. Always trying to tell us how to work. We know how to work. We didn't need some old has-been trying to change our style just because he couldn't keep up."

"Old has-been? Wasn't he the champ?"

"That was Lenny's belt. Mitch was just keeping it warm."

Bennett perked up. "There's Lenny."

Sure enough, Lenny Lambda was heading their way. He hardly looked like a main-event wrestler in his blue Bullseye shirt and khakis, and his normally unruly frosted tips were pulled into a discreet man bun. Ricky Hickson was nowhere in sight, but Lenny was with another Bullseye employee, a heavy-set woman with glasses so thick she could see the future.

Ronnie Hickson waved down his hero. "Hey, Lenny, these little guys want to talk to you."

"Can't you handle it?" The deep, breathy voice Lenny used for his wrestling promos was nowhere to be found, replaced by a higher-pitched lilt common in leprechauns and the like. "Angie needs a refresher on how to use the box compactor."

"Won't take but a minute," Sebastian said. "Just need to ask you a few questions."

Ricky Hickson sprinted in out of nowhere and labored to catch his breath. "Can't find Lenny."

Ronnie Hickson's only response was to point out that Lenny was standing right next to him.

"Oh," Ricky Hickson said. "Hi, Lenny. These two little guys want to talk to you."

"So I've heard. Do me a favor, guys. Show Angie how to work the compactor while I talk to our guests here. And be gentle. She's a bit scared of it."

"C'mon, Angie," Ronnie Hickson said. "There's nothing to be scared of. What are the odds *three* people lose an arm in the same store?"

With that problem solved, Lenny moved on to his next managerial challenge. "What can I do for you guys? But let's keep it quick. I'm an executive, and I have important executive things to do."

"Certainly," Sebastian said. "This is obviously an expertly managed department store, and I would hate to interfere with your official duties. I'll make it brief. My colleague and I are detectives, and we're investigating the—"

"Detectives!"

Lenny let out a schoolgirl squeal and ran away.

Bennett was quick to give chase. "Hurry, Sebastian, he's getting away!"

"More running? These children will be the death of me."

The great chimp detective mustered what energy he could and set after the fleeing suspect. Lenny ran much like he wrestled, ignoring the simplest escape route in favor of overly complicated maneuvers and questionable decisions. He led Bennett and Sebastian through the electronics section, circled back into office supplies, and then raced through home essentials, all the while knocking items off shelves and tossing whatever bathroom products he could grab to impede his pursuers. Bennett had no problems dodging the random projectiles, but a winded Sebastian took a box of Q-tips to the head, reminding him just how dangerous this line of work could be.

Lenny eventually made a break for the emergency exit and slammed through the steel door with a loud *ka-thunk*. Bennett and Sebastian did the same and spotted Lenny across the rear parking lot trying to yank open a battered Toyota Carolla. He raised his hands in surrender.

"Okay, you caught me. But I swear, I only did it the one time."

"That's all it takes to be a murderer," Sebastian said, huffing and wheezing each word. "And was all that running really necessary? I'm too rich to sweat."

"Murderer? I didn't kill anybody."

"Then why were you running?" Bennett asked.

"You mean this isn't about those illegal anime streams?"

"Aniwhat?" Sebastian said. "No, we're looking into the death of Mitch Mayhem. We believe Bonecrusher Brannigan was framed."

"This is wrestling related?" He turned his back to Bennett and Sebastian. With practiced efficiency, he undid the man bun, shook his frosted tips free, and pulled a pair of sunglasses from his pocket. When he turned around, he was no longer Lenny Lambda, Bullseye store manager, but LENNY LAMBDA—WRESTLING SUPERSTAR.

Lenny hooked his thumbs in his pockets and struck a casual-cool pose worthy of a rebellious teenager fresh from detention. He kept his jaw clenched tight as if chewing an imaginary toothpick. "Talk to me."

The transformation confused Sebastian. "You okay? You seem to be having some sort of an episode."

Bennett leaned in and whispered, "It's his character."

Sebastian checked to make sure he was serious. Bennett assured him that he was.

"And what a fine character it is." Placating the delusional was the only way Sebastian got through life. "What do you remember about the night Mitch Mayhem was murdered? Word is you had a fight in the dressing room."

Lenny shifted his weight to his other foot and stared off into the distance, his thrift-store sunglasses obscuring his eyes. "He messed with the puma and got the claws."

"What?"

"He messed with the puma and—"

"No, I heard you. But that's terrible. You don't use that sort of stuff in your promos, do you?"

"He says it all the time," Bennett said.

"What's wrong with it?" Lenny asked, still grunting each word.

"No one talks like that," Sebastian said. "Seems phony. Fans want authenticity, wrestlers who are the same in and out of the ring. And you know that thing you're doing with your voice?"

"Yeah?"

"Stop it."

"Hey, don't tell me how to be a wrestler, and I won't tell you how to be a monkey. Dig?"

"I'm not a monkey, I'm a chimpanzee. But the fact you haven't even brought that up until now is actually refreshing, so I'll let it slide. Just tell me what your issue was with Mitch."

"Didn't like the guy. Said some nasty things about me. And that championship belt was rightfully mine."

"Whoever killed him took the belt. It's still missing."

"Whenever they find it, it's going around my waist."

"Where were you the night he died?"

"After our little scrap with ol' Mitchy Boy, the Hicksons and I needed to blow off some steam, so we picked a few lucky foxes from the crowd and tore up the town."

"That's hard to believe."

"What can I say? The ladies love us."

"I'd like to talk to them."

"Can't. They're from Canada. Just in for the show."

"Pretty sure Canada has phones."

"Forget it. Don't kiss and tell."

"Where did you go? Surely, a waitress or a bartender would remember three famous wrestlers and their dates. They'd confirm your alibi."

"Can't remember."

"Try. It's important."

"I don't know. It was pretty dark."

"What did you have to drink?"

"Beer."

"What kind of beer?"

Lenny hesitated. "Grape?"

"You didn't go out. Ladies don't love you. And you've never had a beer in your life. What are you trying to hide?"

Lenny ripped off his sunglasses and pushed the frosted tips from his face. "Fine. The Hicksons and I went back to my apartment, had some Mountain Dew and Hot Pockets, and played video games all night. They crashed on my couch. Happy?"

"That I can believe."

"Hey, I don't think Crusher did it either. He's a good guy. But I sure as heck didn't do it. And neither did the Hicksons. If I were you, I'd look into Mad Mike Dean. He's a lunatic, always with the barbed-wire weapons and kendo sticks. He had it out for Mitch ever since that botched exploding ring match.”

“I did hear something about that. The explosion was a dud, right?”

“Mad Mike blamed Mitch. Said he sabotaged things to make him look bad. Mitch denied it, but I don’t know. Mitch never liked that death-match stuff. All started because Mad Mike was supposed to get choke-slammed through a car windshield one night, and Mitch wouldn’t let him use real glass.”

“Pretty sure that’s why the Beatles broke up.”

“Never heard of ‘em. Were they a tag team during the territory days?”

“Something like that.”

“Listen, I’m willing to help however I can, but can I please get back to work?” He started to tie his hair into its former bun. “I am an executive after all.”

“Yeah, go ahead.”

A relieved Lenny jogged off toward the main entrance, eager to escape the interrogation.

Sebastian looked to Bennett. “What do you think?”

“Seems to be telling the truth.”

“Does he? People lie a lot. Like, all the time.”

“NiNi says you should never lie.”

“Sound advi—”

“Unless you’re sure you can get away with it.”

“She said that?”

Bennett nodded.

Sebastian started walking him back to the Batmobile. “Might want to keep an eye on that NiNi.”

CHAPTER SIXTEEN

When Bennett and Sebastian made it back to the Batmobile, they found Addie and NiNi standing outside waiting for them.

"We just saw Lenny going in the front door," Addie said, a white plastic shopping bag dangling from her left hand.

"Yeah, we talked to him," Sebastian said.

"Learn anything?" NiNi asked.

"Just that wrestlers aren't what they used to be."

"I could have told you that," Addie said. She shoved the shopping bag into Sebastian's chest. "Here, Monkey. Maybe now you won't look so stupid."

Sebastian looked in the bag. "Jeans?"

"Guessed at the size," NiNi said. "But I'm usually pretty good at that sort of thing."

"And you got these…for *me*?"

"Yeah, I didn't want to," Addie said. "Not sure why you deserve a gift after that dentist trick, but NiNi thought it would be a good idea, so whatever."

"Can't remember the last time anyone got me something. I mean, I'll probably never wear them, and even the thought of denim touching my body makes me a bit queasy, but I appreciate the gesture. Thank you."

"You're welcome," NiNi said. "But you should give them a try. Who knows? You might like it. Now let's get some lunch."

Sebastian suggested jetting off to Paris for proper French cuisine, but he was outvoted, so they just made the short drive down the highway to the Steel Trolley Diner, a local favorite that specialized in greasy goodness. Addie and Bennett liked it because the diner itself looked like an old trolley car. Within minutes, they were perusing their menus in a red vinyl booth—NiNi and Addie on one side and Bennett and Sebastian on the other. Addie and Bennett wanted cheeseburgers, NiNi a garden salad. Sebastian had trouble finding anything worthy of his culinary standards.

A young waitress offered cheerful greeting. "Hi, my name is Bethany, and I'll be your server today. If you're in the mood for dessert, the special is banana cream pie, and we—"

Sebastian, who to this point had been hidden from view, slammed his menu down on the table. "Oh, I see. Because I'm a *monkey*," he made air quotes with his fingers to drive home the point, "I must want the banana cream pie, is that it?"

"I didn't…I mean, I had no—"

"Give the dumb monkey a banana, that'll make him happy. Here, monkey, monkey. Want a banana? Come get your banana like a good little monkey."

"Calm down, Sebastian," NiNi said. "She was just telling us the dessert specials. She didn't mean to offend you."

"No, no, of course not," Bethany said. "I would never—"

"But you did, *Bethany*," Sebastian said. "Look how I'm dressed? Do I look like a common monkey? I'll have you know that I have a very educated palate that goes far beyond mere bananas. I am a chimpanzee of culture and refinement, and I deserve to be treated as such."

Addie blew the paper from her drinking straw across the table at Sebastian. "Aw, relax, Monkey. I'm sure she's sorry."

"Yes, I apologize, sir," Bethany said, her hand over her heart. "Really. I am so sorry."

Sebastian studied her a moment to weigh her contrition. "Forgiven. This time."

NiNi ordered for the others, and Bethany seemed extra careful to make sure that she had each item correct, dutifully noting that

Bennett preferred tater-tots to french fries. After putting it off as long as possible, she timidly asked Sebastian, "Have you decided, sir?"

"It all looks so repugnant. But you know what? I'm not that hungry." He returned his menu to its rightful stand at the rear of the table. "I'll just have a slice of the banana cream pie. Thank you."

Bethany gave Sebastian a look dirtier than a worm's belly before leaving.

"She's so gonna spit in your pie," Addie said.

"Nonsense. Bethany is a professional, and the customer is always right. And that is especially true when I am the customer. But before our food gets here, I think it's time I give you another detective lesson."

Addie and Bennett sat up like star pupils, eager to learn more of the great chimp detective's wisdom.

"Might want to listen up, NiNi," Addie said. "As stupid as he is, these are actually pretty good. Go ahead, Monkey. Whatta ya got?"

Sebastian folded his hands on the table and adopted a professorial air. "When conducting an extensive investigation, it is critical to periodically review the information you have gathered to determine exactly what you know and what must still be learned. It often helps to have a sounding board or colleagues with whom to discuss these details. My father and Sidney used to perform that role for me. Since there are no other suitable replacements, you will suffice. Who would you say is our chief suspect?"

"Jill," Addie said.

"Why?"

"She's a dentist."

"I'm afraid we need more than that. She does have motive due to her former relationship with Mitch and his blackmailing her, but she doesn't strike me as the murdering type. If she were, she likely would have killed Mitch long ago. The timing of his death—coming just hours after he publicly aired his grievances with several co-workers—and the missing championship belt would seem to indicate that the root issue was related to professional jealousy."

"I don't know," Addie said, shaking her impish head. "Dentists are pretty, pretty sneaky."

"I think it was Mad Mike Dean," Bennett said. "Lenny told us that Mad Mike blamed Mitch for the ring not exploding."

NiNi asked, "And that's a bad thing?"

"When you're supposed to have an exploding ring match, NiNi," Addie said, "and the ring doesn't explode, yeah, it's a bad thing. Hilarious, but still bad."

"And we know Mad Mike is crazy," Bennett said. "Look how rough he was with you, Sebastian."

NiNi said, "He got rough with you?"

Sebastian fiddled with the cuffs of his smoking jacket. "Nothing I couldn't handle."

"Should have seen it, NiNi," Addie said, unable to suppress her glee. "Mad Mike dumped Monkey out the door like a bag of garbage. It was so awesome."

"I remember it differently," Sebastian said. "But Dean does have the temperament to be a killer, and crushing Mitch's skull with a blunt object certainly aligns with his caveman-like tendencies. But why would he care about the championship belt? He doesn't strike me as someone who values championships and personal accolades, unless they come wrapped in barbed wire."

"We know Lenny cares about winning the championship," Bennett said. "And Mitch refused to even wrestle him. After they had their fight in the dressing room, Mitch told Lenny that he'd never get his hands on the belt."

Addie thumped her fist on the table. "So he bashed Mitch over the head and took it."

"Doubtful," Sebastian said. "The guy Bennett and I just talked to doesn't seem tough enough to kill anyone."

"He could have been acting," Bennett said. "He's very theatrical."

"Yeah, he pretends he's a wrestler all the time," Addie said, laughing at her own joke.

"Or maybe the Hicksons killed Mitch for Lenny," Bennett said. "They'd do anything for him."

"I question whether they can tie their own shoes," Sebastian said. "I suspect murder might be beyond their capabilities."

"If it wasn't the Hicksons, maybe someone else killed Mitch for him. Lenny has a lot of crazy fans."

"Yeah, you'd have to be crazy to like that guy," Addie said. "And internet wrestling fans are the worst. They all read the Squared Circle. Bunch of crybabies who think Lenny should be champ."

"I vote for Manero," NiNi said. "I think I can still smell that creep's cologne."

"And we know he was feeding stories to the dirt sheets to make Mitch look bad," Bennett said. "Plus, at his age, he probably wasn't going to get another shot at the title."

Addie thumped her fist on the table again, louder this time. "So he bashed Mitch over the head and took it."

Sebastian's brows furrowed with concentration. "Perhaps."

"But we can't forget about Tony," Bennett said. "That dressing room fight ruined his TV deal. And Tony's father told us he could be cutting off the money soon."

"Money is always a good motive for murder," NiNi said.

"And Mitch was refusing to lose. Tony had to get the belt back."

Addie thumped the table a third time. "So he bashed Mitch over the head and—wait a minute. Tiny's a wimp. No way he could have cracked Mitch's melon."

"Yes," Sebastian said, "Tony committing murder, particularly one by way of blunt force trauma, seems highly unlikely. All things considered, I would say it's down to Mad Mike Dean, Manero, and Lenny."

"What's our next move?" Addie said.

"I think it would be wise to pay Steve Thacker another visit. Now that we know Manero was indeed his source for the anti-Mitch stories, perhaps we can leverage that for more information."

Sebastian spied Bethany coming out of the kitchen with their food. "But first, we feast. Then we hunt."

Over lunch, Sebastian regaled them with tales of his past adventures, including the time he recovered a collection of rare coins worth over eight million dollars. That particular case involved deep-sea diving, two sword fights, and a hot air balloon chase. While impressed with Sebastian's stories, NiNi seemed more delighted with the smiles on her grandchildren's faces, a rare sight since their father's arrest. Sebastian insisted on paying the check, and he even gave Bethany an extremely generous tip. A good time was had by all.

The merriment continued on the way out of the diner, with Addie and Bennett arguing over who had the better elbow drop, Shawn Michaels or Macho Man Randy Savage. Sebastian followed his colleagues out the door before hesitating.

"What's wrong?" NiNi asked, a grandchild at each hip.

"I hate to admit it, but that pie was scrumptious. I think I'm going to see if I can get a whole one to go."

"Hurry up, Monkey," Addie said. "We've got a case to solve."

"We'll be waiting," NiNi said.

Sebastian couldn't help but smile at the sight of NiNi, an arm around each grandchild, chaperoning her charges across the parking lot toward the Batmobile. That's when he heard the revving engine.

It all happened so fast.

Whether animal instinct or his years of crime-fighting experience, Sebastain sensed something was wrong. A white van shot from a spot on the right side of the parking lot and zoomed toward NiNi and the kids. Sebastian yelled for them to look out, but the warning only made them stop and look at him. He was already in full gallop, his fine Italian loafers and powerful primate palms propelling him forward like a hairy rocket. He stretched his arms wide and launched into them with the explosiveness of an All-Pro linebacker, sending everyone tumbling backward across the asphalt just before the speeding van raced by and merged onto the highway, its escape met with honking horns and screeching tires.

NiNi made it up to her knees. "Is everyone okay?"

"Whoa, Monkey," Addie said, still lying on the concrete. "I didn't know you could run like that. You're a superhero."

"Yeah, you saved our lives, Sebastian," Bennett said. He seemed no worse for wear and was helping NiNi to her feet. "Do you think that had to do with the case?"

"It is a distinct possibility," Sebastian said, although he was more concerned with the unsightly scuffs on his khakis. His wardrobe was not meant for tackling. "And if it were intentional, it proves that your father is innocent and that the real killer is still on the loose. Unfortunately, I didn't get a good look at the driver. All I saw was sunglasses and a hood pulled up over a ballcap. But whoever it was had to have followed us here."

"Maybe it was one of the Hickson Brothers?" Bennett said. "They could have snuck out while we were talking to Lenny."

Addie got to her feet. "Could have been Dean. He's got plumbing vans like that."

"And Manero has a used car lot. He could have a van."

"C'mon, Monkey. Time's a wastin'. Let's get after 'em."

"Hold it," NiNi said. "This has been fun and all, but if that really was intentional, this might be getting a bit too dangerous for you two. I think it might be time to let Sebastian handle things on his own."

"You've seen Monkey," Addie said. "He's helpless without us. We can't just—ooh." The color drained from her face.

"What's wrong?"

"My wrist hurts."

"Let me see." NiNi carefully inspected Addie's left wrist, feeling for any breaks. "Can you move it?"

Her eyes grew wide, and she let out a sharp, "Yeowww!"

NiNi frowned. "I'm afraid our next stop is the emergency room."

CHAPTER SEVENTEEN

The Batmobile pulled in front of the Pajakowski houshold. The mood of its passengers was far more somber than it had been earlier in the day—three hours at the emergency room will do that. There was also the impending doom of having to inform Addie and Bennett's mother about their recent adventures with Sebastian, including Addie's broken wrist. NiNi had elected not to call their mother at work. After all, the injury wasn't that serious, and NiNi thought sparing her daughter the worry of an unexpected hospital visit would be the considerate thing to do. Plus, it would avoid Michelle yelling at her in public for being irresponsible and untrustworthy, which seemed to be a recurring theme in their relationship. Addie knew her mother would be upset, but she was no stranger to trouble, so she wasn't too worried. Bennett was the one taking it the hardest, and he still had two functioning wrists. He was supposed to look after his little sister. He was supposed to be the responsible one. But the neon pink cast on Addie's left arm proved otherwise. Even Sebastian was apprehensive about meeting with Addie and Bennett's mother. Sure, he had matinee-idol good looks and rapier-like wit, but being forgiven for breaking a child's wrist, particularly when the injury occurred while saving said child from an even worse fate, could test his admirable charms.

Yet a sliver of curiosity pierced the palpable dread. They had expected to arrive home to an empty house, where they would stew in anxious misery until their mother arrived home from work around six o'clock. However, NiNi had to park in front of the house because two cars already occupied the driveway: their mother's blue Honda Civic and an unknown silver Lexus.

The mystery deepened when they entered the house and heard their mother's laughter coming from the kitchen. Why was she laughing? She never laughed. There was also another voice. A man's voice. They were having such a good time that neither one had heard the door.

Perhaps uncertain as to what they had interrupted, NiNi announced their arrival. "Michelle, I brought the kids home a little early."

"Mom?"

There were a few hushed words, and then Addie and Bennett's mother appeared in the kitchen doorway. She was dressed in her work outfit of a white blouse and gray pencil skirt, and she was the picture of paralegal perfection. The surprising thing was that a tall, handsome blond-haired man in a dark brown suit loomed behind her. He looked like he had just stepped out of a shampoo commercial. Their mother seemed a bit flustered, but any uncomfortableness in her manner disappeared when she caught sight of Addie's pink cast. Now there was only concern.

"What happened to your arm?"

"I broke it," Addie said. "Who's this clown?"

Her mother rushed over and knelt next to Addie to survey the damage. "My poor baby. Are you okay?" She fired an angry look at NiNi. "Why didn't you call me?"

"I didn't want to disturb you at work. It's a tiny little fracture. She'll be good as new in a few weeks."

"What happened?"

"You should have seen it, Mommy," Addie said. "This van was coming right for us, and it was going like a hundred miles an hour, but Sebastian knocked us out of the way just in time. Must have hurt my wrist when we fell."

Her mother was horrified. "Someone tried to run you over?"

"Yeah, but there was nothing to worry about. Sebastian saved us."

"Who's Sebastian?"

The great chimp detective cleared his throat and stepped out from behind NiNi. "It's a pleasure to meet you, Mrs. Pajakowski. Or should I call you Michelle? I am the Sebastian in question. Sebastian Winthrop, chimp detective. And by that I mean I am a chimp who is a detective, not that I only investigate chimps. Addie and Bennett have procured my services to prove your husband's innocence. And despite today's unfortunate events, I truly believe we are getting closer to that objective."

Their mother was stunned stupid. She stared in silence at Sebastian until her brain rebooted. "Why is there a talking monkey in my house?"

"He's a chimp," Bennett said.

"I most certainly am." Sebastian walked past Mrs. Pajakowski and greeted the unknown man. "Don't think we've had the pleasure, good sir. Sebastian Winthrop. And you are?"

The man shook Sebastian's hand the way one tests if a bath is too hot. "Don Troutman. I work at the law firm with Mich, er, Mrs. Pajakowski."

Michelle stood and provided further explanation. "Don is helping with Daddy's case."

"Sounded like you were having a good old time doing it too," Addie said, glowering at Don Troutman.

"We should exchange notes," Sebastian said. "Our investigation has produced quite a few promising leads, any one of which could be enough to establish reasonable doubt. Let me know if you need help drafting the defense. I can think of at least three Perry Mason episodes that may provide a strategic blueprint."

"Wait," Michelle said, "you're telling me that you hired a monkey detective behind my back, and because you have been running around town investigating a murder, you ended up breaking your wrist after nearly being run over by a van?"

Addie shrugged. "More or less."

"And you knew about this?" The question and its accompanying icy stare were directed at NiNi.

"We were just trying to help."

"You lied to me. Again!"

Don Troutman eased toward the exit. "This seems like a family matter, so maybe I should just—"

"Not so fast, counselor," said a new but familiar voice. Everyone turned to see Chief Bouchard, Canadian tuque and all, filling the front doorway. "I think you're gonna want to stick around for this."

CHAPTER EIGHTEEN

"Well, if it isn't Chief Dominique Bouchard," Sebastian said. "Who ordered the Canadian bacon?"

"Very funny, Monkey," Chief Bouchard said. "A real laugh riot you are. But we'll see who's laughing here in a minute, eh." He galumphed in like he owned the place, not even bothering to wipe his shoes. He handed Addie and Bennett's mother a folded piece of paper. "Mrs. Pajakowski, this here is a search warrant for the premises."

Michelle gave the warrant a quick read and then passed it off to Don Troutman. "Haven't we done this before?"

"Let's just say some new information has come to light."

"Like what?"

"Just you wait and see. Shouldn't be long." Chief Bouchard hitched up his pants and sidled over to NiNi. "How've you been, Val? You look sweeter than a box of Timbits." He looked back at Sebastian. "Those are tasty little donuts in Canada. I know that because I was born in Canada."

"Been better, Dom," NiNi said, crossing her arms. "Don't know if you've heard, but some dummies arrested my son-in-law for murder."

"You know each other?" Sebastian asked.

"Val and I went to high school together," Chief Bouchard said. "Shame to see she's hanging around with mangy zoo animals."

"Those are her grandchildren, you twit. Please do not disrespect them in my presence."

"Thanks, Monkey," Addie said.

"No problem. But since you're here, Chief, I should let you know that I am more convinced than ever that their father is innocent. Not only that, I believe we are closing in on identifying the true killer."

"Is that right?"

"Should have the case solved in a matter of days."

"That's funny. Because I think I'll have it closed in about, oh, five seconds."

The Chief nodded to the front door, causing the white pompom on his crimson tuque to dance. A uniformed officer entered the house carrying a green duffle bag smudged with dirt. He presented the bag to Chief Bouchard, and clumps of soil and bits of grass dropped to the floor, further marring the Pajakowski carpeting. "Right where you said it would be."

"Thank you, Jimmy." The Chief unzipped the bag. "We got an anonymous tip. A neighbor said they saw someone digging in the backyard on the night Mitch was murdered. Told us to look under the birdbath. And what do you think we found?" He reached into the bag and pulled out the missing KCW Heavyweight Championship. Demonstrating a complete disregard for forensic evidence, he slapped the belt across his shoulder and posed like a proud champion. "Hey, look at me, Monkey. I won."

The room went deathly silent. Seeing the gold-plated belt on Chief Bouchard's shoulder forced everyone to confront a harsh reality: Stanley Pajakowski—loving husband, devoted father, and dutiful son-in-law—was guilty.

Addie screamed, "But Daddy didn't do it! Tell him, Monkey. Tell him Daddy didn't do it."

For the first time in forever, Sebastian was uncertain what to say. The championship being unearthed in the Pajakowski backyard was certainly an unexpected development. However, it all seemed a bit too convenient. "Clearly, your anonymous tipster put the belt there. That individual is the guilty party, and if we—"

"Enough!" Michelle Pajakowski closed her eyes. "I would like everyone to leave."

"That's fine," Chief Bouchard said. "We're done here anyway." He strolled out with the belt on his shoulder and a spring in his step.

Don Troutman placed a reassuring hand on Michelle's lower back. "Call me if you need anything."

She thanked him and said she'd see him at work.

Addie gave Troutman the skunk eye on his way out the door and then renewed the battle. "Mom, listen to Monkey. We can—"

"Addie, please."

"But you know Daddy didn't do it. You can't just—"

"Addie, shut up! Your little investigation is over. It's all over. I don't want to hear another word out of you, got it? Nothing about your stupid monkey detective. Nothing about how Daddy's innocent. Nothing. Not a peep. And if I do, a broken wrist will be the least of your problems. Now go to your room!"

Addie let out a frustrated scream, which technically wasn't a word, and stormed off. She made sure to slam her bedroom door.

"Michelle, calm down," NiNi said. "There's no reason to yell at Addie."

"Spare me the parenting advice. Or should I just lie to them like you always do to me? Yeah, that's right, kids. Daddy's innocent. Life's great. We're not gonna lose the house. And we won't be known as that crazy killer's family. Nope. Not at all. Everything's going to be wonderful. How's that? Is that better?"

Bennett wiped a tear from his cheek and took off running for his bedroom.

"Benny, I'm sorry, I didn't—" She spun back around to NiNi. "Look what you made me do!"

"You did that on your own."

"Get out of my house. I mean it. Get out. I don't need you filling my kids' heads with fantasies. I don't need you giving them hope for some storybook ending that isn't going to happen. In fact, I don't need you, period."

NiNi calmly turned and walked out the front door. "Call me when you get ahold of yourself."

"Don't wait up."

Michelle slammed the door. NiNi waited patiently. A few seconds later, the door opened, Sebastian got shoved outside, and then the door slammed again.

The world was eerily quiet in contrast to the madhouse they had just left. What an ugly, ugly scene it was.

"Anyhoo," Sebastian said. "Want to get some Chinese food?"

NiNi stalked off toward the Batmobile.

"Too soon?"

CHAPTER NINETEEN

NiNi pulled the Batmobile behind Ol' Blue and cut the engine. The brief thirty-second ride back from Addie and Bennett's house was spent in silence. But before NiNi opened her door, Sebastian summoned the courage to ask a personal question.

"What's the deal with you and Michelle?"

"It's a long story."

"I've got time."

She drummed her thumbs on the steering wheel, debating how to begin. "I had her when I was very young. And let's just say her father wasn't someone I was proud of or really even liked. Just one of those things, you know? He wasn't someone I wanted in my life, let alone my child's. And it's not like he was jumping up and down to be a father either. Getting married would have just made things worse, so I raised Michelle with the help of my grandmother in this very house, and we made the best of things. Along the way, I maybe led Michelle to believe that her father was dead."

"How'd you do that?"

"I think I said something like, 'Your father's dead.' And I may have possibly invented an entire backstory for him and even made annual visits to a gravesite. It was a whole thing."

"Oh."

"It started out innocently enough but just kind of spiraled out of control. I thought I was doing the right thing. I mean, I was trying to protect her and give her a father she could be proud of." She added in a reverent tone, "Trevor was a doctor."

Sebastian winced. "Of all the names you could have picked for her fake father, you chose Trevor?"

"What's wrong with Trevor?"

"Sounds like a weenie."

"Hardly. I'll have you know he was a real man's man. Wrestled in high school. Boxed. Sure, he liked his scotch a bit too much, but he had a tough upbringing in the orphanage, and his job was so stressful. Had his plane not gone down over the Amazon while on that humanitarian mission, he would have been a wonderful father."

"And Michelle bought all this?"

"Oh yeah, kids are stupid. But the point is she thought her dad was dead. Until he wasn't."

"How'd she find out?"

"Ran into him at a high school football game."

"And I take it he's not a doctor?"

"Unless you count unemployed bum as a medical profession. Needless to say, my relationship with Michelle was downhill from there. And then she pretty much repeated all my same mistakes, except she married Bennett and Addie's dad. I've been able to get back into her good graces over the years by helping with the kids. But we still tend to be up and down. She'll go off on me every so often, but she usually calms down after a few days, typically when she needs a babysitter. The joys of parenting."

NiNi exited the vehicle, and Sebastian followed suit. The only activity on the street was the rhythmic spitting of a neighboring yard sprinkler and the occasional chirps of playful sparrows.

"Always thought Stan was a good guy," NiNi said, resting her back on the railing of her front porch steps. "Not the sharpest tool in the shed, but a good guy. Until all this."

"I wouldn't worry too much about that belt. It was obviously placed there to incriminate him."

"Maybe."

"Don't forget about the van that tried to run you down."

"Could have just been a lousy driver."

"You really believe that?"

"I don't know what to believe anymore."

"Buck up. We'll get to the bottom of this yet. Meet here at nine a.m. tomorrow?"

"That's probably not a good idea."

"You're right. Without the kiddos around, there's no need to rush. Let's make it noonish."

"No, Sebastian, I mean I can't keep investigating things with you."

"Why not? You're a natural."

"No offense, but Michelle seems to hate you. And she made it pretty clear she doesn't want us giving the kids false hope. If she ever found out I was still helping you, that really might be it for me. But if I just lay low and stay out of trouble, she'll calm down in a few days, and everything will go back to normal." She walked up the porch steps. When she reached the top, she turned and looked back at Sebastian. "But, hey, thanks for everything. Today was really fun…except for when I almost got killed and had my daughter disown me."

Sebastian gazed up at her. The distance between them, no more than five porch steps, seemed insurmountable. "So that's it?"

"For now at least, yeah. But I'm sure I'll see you around."

"How?"

The question went unanswered. She gave him a gentle wave goodbye before going inside and shutting the door.

Sebastian stood there a moment, his lip quivering and his heart heavy, hoping the door would open again.

It did not.

CHAPTER TWENTY

The next few days were a blur.

Sebastian quickly settled into his old routine of napping, not leaving the house, and napping some more. In one of his rare conscious moments, he did check the local news and read about the police finding the missing championship belt, all but condemning Bonecrusher Brannigan to life behind bars. The trial date was fast approaching. Tony Katsaros also announced that his next event would feature a triple-threat match between Vince Manero, Mad Mike Dean, and Lenny Lambda for the recovered KCW Heavyweight Championship. Tickets were going fast.

Sebastian didn't care. He was relieved to be done with the whole mess. No more annoying kids bothering him. No more dealing with people. No more feeling hurt ever again. He just wanted to be left alone.

He pulled tight his weighted blanket and curled up in his luxuriously comfortable bed in his cozy, safe bedroom, the delightfully familiar sounds of a *Columbo* episode lulling him to sleep. So what if the cops arrested the wrong man? The courts would decide the matter. Wasn't his problem. Either way, Addie and Bennett would be fine. Their mother would take good care of them, and NiNi was always around. Better that they learn life wasn't fair early on. Toughen them up. Make them resistant to future heartaches. Yes, everything worked out for the best.

Sebastian closed his eyes and listened to the TV show's dialogue. It was an old relaxation trick he had for falling asleep. He found that repeating each line of dialogue in his head helped quiet his mind, enabling him to obtain peaceful slumber. He was several lines into the calming technique when he heard Lieutenant Columbo utter his famous, "Just one more thing." Sebastian repeated it over and over. Just one more thing. Just one more thing.

He shot up in bed, wide awake and alert.

He couldn't let it end like this. He was a detective! Whether Addie and Bennett's mother wanted him investigating the case was immaterial. This was a matter of professional pride. The only thing necessary for evil to win was for good chimps to do nothing. Sure, the world was awash in corruption, and the media and elite globalists conspired to keep the peasants dumb, distracted, and drugged. Truth had no chance against such overwhelming opposition. But a good detective had a moral code. He may not be able to win the war, but he could win this battle. Right here, right now, he could take a stand. He could do what was right. He could defend truth and free an innocent man. Besides, he couldn't just forsake Bennett. The poor lad was too sensitive for this world. He had to be protected at all costs. And what about Addie? If left unchecked, she could wreak untold havoc and bring down whatever semblance of civil society still existed. Yes, the world needed him.

They needed him.

But first, Sebastian needed a nap. Spiritual epiphanies were exhausting.

CHAPTER TWENTY-ONE

Addie had been dreaming that a giant purple squirrel was dropping acorns on her head. The acorns didn't hurt, but they made the most annoying *tap* sound whenever they plunked off her skull and hit the floor. And for some reason, the stupid squirrel was wearing a smoking jacket. One particularly plump acorn made such a loud tapping noise that she actually woke up. Her room was dark, except for the warm glow of her unicorn nightlight, and she immediately became aware of the heavy cast on her arm. She adjusted her covers, intent on getting back to sleep as quickly as possible so she could give that squirrel a punch in the belly.

Tap, tap, tap.

She was awake. Why was she still hearing the tapping?

Tap, tap, tap.

Man, that squirrel was a real jerk. She rolled over to go back to sleep, but the drapes were parted just enough to reveal a grinning face outside her window. If it were a burglar, he certainly liked his job. He was also short. And hairy.

"Monkey!"

Addie leapt out of bed and raced to the window. She ripped open the drapes to find Sebastian waving at her. She waved back and then opened the window, which wasn't so easy with a broken wrist.

"About time you got here. Mom took our phones and hasn't been letting us use the internet. Says we're grounded for the rest of the summer. She also got some mean old lady to babysit us. You should see her, she's even older than NiNi."

Sebastian climbed in the window. "Sounds horrific. How's Bennett doing?"

"He's okay. Just been reading his dumb books. But at least it keeps him out of my hair."

"And the wrist?"

"Cast gets itchy. But I feel like Cowboy Bob Orton on the lead-up to WrestleMania I." She swung her arm like a club. "So that's pretty cool. But I'm glad you're here. Don't listen to my mom, I want you back on the case."

"Never left it. I may have taken a brief respite to get some much needed rest, but I assure you, I am still working on it."

"You're really earning those cookies."

Sebastian took a seat on the foot of the bed, and Addie joined him.

"I had Detective Carter check all the suspects' driving records and vehicle registrations. Dean has the plumbing vans, but they've all got the company logo. No other plain white vans. I tried various rental companies around town. Came up empty."

"That stinks. What else you got?"

"You may not have heard, but Tony is having a triple-threat match for the title this weekend."

"Dean, Lambda, and Manero?"

"Correct."

"Daddy is way better than all of 'em. Can't believe he's still stuck in jail while those bums get to wrestle for the title. It's not fair, Monkey. None of this is fair."

"Agreed."

Addie stared at the floor. "Hey, Monkey?"

"Yeah."

"Can I tell you a secret?"

"Sure."

"Gotta promise not to tell anyone, especially Bennett."

"Promise."

"Remember when Bennett and I first met you, and I cried to get you to take the case?" She hesitated. "The tears were real."

Sebastian pulled Addie against him in a one-armed hug. "I know."

She rested her head on his shoulder, and they sat quietly, taking comfort in no longer feeling quite so alone.

Finally, after a respectful amount of time, Sebastian said, "Hey, Addie?"

"Yeah?"

"Remember when I said you were a loud-mouthed little twerp who never shuts up?"

"Uh-huh."

"I meant it."

Addie smiled. "I know."

The wholesome moment ended when Addie beheld something miraculous. She hadn't realized it at first because of the darkness, but there was just enough illumination from her nightlight to reveal the incredible.

"Monkey, you're wearing jeans!"

"Thought it was time to try something new."

"Well, what do you think?"

Sebastian stretched out his legs to admire the denim. "Gotta say, they make me feel pretty tough."

"There's hope for you yet. Now we just have to lose the smoking jackets."

"Yeah, that will never happen. But we still have a case to solve."

"You're right. First we save Daddy, then we save your closet."

"The upcoming championship match seems like a perfect opportunity. All the key players will be there. All we have to do is apply the proper pressure at the right moment, and the case will break wide open."

"Okay, but how do we do that?"

The bedroom lights burst to life. Sebastian spun to discover Addie's mother standing in the doorway. And she was not amused.

CHAPTER TWENTY-TWO

Even in her bulky blue bathrobe, Addie's mother cut a petite figure. Yet in that moment, Sebastian found her more frightening than Godzilla, King Kong, or smiling politicians.

"What is *he* doing here?"

Addie jumped between them. "Mommy, Sebastian is here to help. If you'd just give him a chance, he's gonna prove Daddy's innocent."

"I told you I didn't want you hanging around with him anymore. For all we know, he could have monkeypox."

Sebastian, in the most polite tone he could marshal after being so grievously insulted, said, "Mrs. Pajakowski, I can assure you that I—" Now that the lights were on, Addie's bedroom was unveiled, creating quite the distraction. The walls were a pale purple and featured decorative rainbows, hearts, and unicorns. The white wooden dressers in the corners opposite the bed were surprisingly neat and orderly. An assortment of stuffed animals, mostly cuddly teddy bears or fluffy bunnies, occupied a chair next to the bed, and even the bedding was an array of pinks and purples. "This is your room?"

"What of it?" Addie said over her shoulder, her attention entirely on her mother.

"Not what I expected. What with all the hearts and bunnies and whatnot."

Addie turned to face him. "What's wrong with bunnies?"

"Oh, nothing."

"Addie," her mother said, "I can't have you investigating murders with a monkey detective. It's dangerous, and you could even ruin potential evidence or—"

Addie waved her off like a persistent gnat. "Yeah, yeah, whatever. What's wrong with my room, Monkey?"

"It's a perfectly fine room."

"Addie…."

"In a minute, Mommy. Go ahead, Monkey. Say it."

Sebastian scratched his head, debating how to best handle the situation. Then he remembered his recent recommitment to the truth. "I mean, it's just a little soft, no?"

"Soft?"

"Little bit."

"I'll show you soft…."

She raised her cast, but her mother wrapped her up tight. "Addie, you can't hit someone with your broken wrist."

"Listen to your mother," Sebastian said.

"Kick him instead."

Any potential chimp kicking got postponed when Bennett ran into the room.

"Sebastian!"

He raced right past his mother and sister to give the great monkey detective a big hug. Sebastian returned the embrace.

"What are you doing here?" Bennett asked. "Did you solve the case?"

"Not yet. But we're close. I'm hoping I can have your mother's blessing to continue the investigation."

Addie and Bennett's mother collapsed on Addie's bed, her spirit broken. "My husband is in jail for murder. My kids hate me. I can't trust my mother. Then there's all that stuff with Don at work. I mean, I don't want to have an affair, do I? And now I'm arguing with a talking monkey."

Bennett raised his hand. "What was that thing about Don?"

Addie put her good arm around her mother. "We don't hate you, Mommy. We love you. So does NiNi. And sure, Monkey is annoying, and he's too fancy for his own good, but he's the best detective in the world. If you'd just let us help, we'll prove Daddy is innocent."

Addie's mother looked at her. "You mean it?"

"Oh yeah, Monkey is super deluxe annoying."

"Not that. You guys still love me?"

Addie and Bennett both hugged their mother, and the weeks of fear and anxiety seemed to fade. Sebastian was so moved by the emotional display, he spread his arms wide and tried to get in on the group hug. Addie and Bennett welcomed him in, but their mother stopped him with a stern glare.

"Solve the case first," she said.

"Fair enough." Sebastian lifted his chin. "Thankfully, there is no off position on the genius switch. And after considering all the angles, I can confidently state that...I have a plan."

CHAPTER TWENTY-THREE

The bingo hall was rocking. A sold-out crowd had showed up to witness a truly historic wrestling event. Billed as Brawl Out, the card featured six brutal matches, including Jill Johnson defending the Women's Championship against the dastardly Devon St. Denis, and the Hickson Brothers putting the Tag Team Titles on the line against the Grave Stompers. But, of course, the match that drew the house was the main event: Vince Manero, Mad Mike Dean, and Lenny Lambda in a triple-threat clash for the KCW Heavyweight Championship.

Tony Katsaros, the man responsible for it all, stood at the backstage curtain and marveled at his own creative brilliance. As much as he would have liked to finish watching the Hickson Brothers' match, which would end with a finish only someone of his astute wrestling pedigree could devise, there was still work to be done. He closed the curtain and headed back toward the dressing room to give the main-eventers their final instructions. This would be his crowning achievement as a booker, shepherding the fledgling promotion from tragedy to triumph, paying tribute to the departed Mitch Mayhem while still managing to anoint a new champion. No one else in the history of professional wrestling could have crafted such a perfect transition, of that he was certain. He hoped the fans knew how lucky they were.

Jill Johnson exited the women's dressing room. She had swapped her white and gold wrestling gear for jeans and a sweater, and Tony nearly swooned when he saw her smiling at him.

"You really liked the match?" she said. "You're not just saying that to make me feel good, right?"

"No, no, you were great. One of your best title defenses yet." Tony went in for a hug, but Jill turned away, not even noticing his inept advance. He played it cool though and pretended he was just stretching.

"Do you think anyone caught the little slip-up on the piledriver?"

"Can't see how. You hid it like a true pro."

"That's a relief. Maybe Thacker will still give me five stars."

"By the way, how's Devon doing?"

"She's got feeling back in her legs, and I think she's real close to remembering her name. But hey, I'm gonna go get ready to watch the main event. Can't wait to see what you cooked up."

Tony's second attempt at physical contact fell flatter than the first. Jill had already turned to leave, so he just ended up hugging the air and imagining what their children would look like. The only thing that ended his reverie was the sound of the metal exit door opening at the other end of the hall.

In walked a petite brunette in a charcoal gray business suit. Her hair was pulled back tight, and she stepped with confidence, her heels clacking against the hallway's tile flooring with piston-like precision. Flanking her on either side were two masked wrestlers wearing matching blue spandex bodysuits with red trunks and boots. Their masks were also blue, the eyes, noses, and mouths outlined in red. Both wrestlers were smaller than the woman. The one on the right, the slightly taller of the two, was thin-boned and struggled to carry the steel attaché case at his side, the extra weight knocking him off-kilter. He also wore round spectacles over his mask. The wrestler on the left had a bright pink cast on one arm, the true sign of a rough customer. It wasn't until they got closer that Tony realized there was a fourth member of the party. The mystery man was almost entirely obscured from view, with only flashes of a blue sequined cape betraying his presence.

"Mr. Tony Katsaros?" the woman in the business suit said above the muffled cheers of the crowd.

"Can I help you?"

"I'm Cagney N. Lacey, and I represent the interests of Rockford, Mannix, Starsky, and Hutch, a global hedge fund that has investments in such wide-ranging industries as pumpkin farming, llama racing, and potato-powered clocks. I would like to discuss with you a most attractive business proposition."

Tony craned his neck but still couldn't get a good look at the blue-caped individual. "I'm sorry, but I can't talk now. Our main event is about to start in like five minutes, and I need to make sure everything is ready to go." Tony tried to leave, but the wee wrestler with the pink cast barked at him, causing him to jump back in fright.

"We are aware of the time constraints, Mr. Katsaros," the businesswoman said. "We planned to be here earlier, but I suppose I don't have to tell you about the nuisance of private jet travel. I'll be brief. Rockford, Mannix, Starsky, and Hutch has branched out into professional wrestling, and we have acquired the IWO, a popular Mexican promotion. However, our goal is American expansion, and we would like to work with KCW. In short, we want to be in your main event."

Tony laughed. "I've scripted the perfect triple threat. There are way too many moving parts. I can't just add someone to the match."

"Mr. Katsaros, I am offering you the opportunity to be a cornerstone of our American expansion. We have already secured a major deal with a popular streaming network. I am not at liberty to divulge the name of said network, but let's just say it rhymes with Shmetflix. All we're asking is that you help raise our profile in the States by including one of our biggest superstars in your main event."

"Can't we talk about this after the show? We could set something up for next week."

She shook her head with grim conviction. "It must be today. If you cannot accommodate us, we will simply find another partner."

"But I don't think you understand how difficult it is to change a three-way match into a fatal four-way."

The woman took the shiny steel briefcase from her masked colleague.

"I mean, my performers are true professionals. I couldn't possibly spring such major changes on them at the last minute."

She placed the briefcase on her outstretched left forearm and used her right hand to manipulate the latches.

"And what about the fans? They bought tickets to see a triple threat. That's what they want, and that's what I'm going to give them. I'm sorry, but it's out of the question."

The woman lifted the briefcase lid.

Tony gulped.

"Do we have a deal?"

The case was filled with stacks and stacks of cold hard cash, enough money to finally make the promotion profitable. He wouldn't even need his dad's help this time. "Would you like all three of them in the match? I'm sure we could work around the broken arm. Shouldn't be a problem."

"You've made the right choice."

She shut the briefcase and handed it to Tony. He clutched it to his chest with more enthusiasm than his imaginary Jill hugs.

"Mr. Katsaros, allow me to introduce the Tres Terrores, the hottest lucha libre trios team in all of Mexico." She informed him that the one with the pink cast was named Ladrona, and the bespectacled one was Bandito. "But the individual who will be representing us in your main event will be…El Mono Diablo!"

She stepped aside with a flourish, and the third luchador squared up with raised fists. He had an identical mask and a similar blue-and-red outfit as the others, although he wore a sequined cape— the lining of which was red—and his blue spandex top featured a deep-scooped neck and exposed arms, showing off an outlandishly hairy torso.

"Whoa," Tony said. "Don't they have razors in Mexico? But it's okay. No one has done the body hair gimmick since George 'The Animal' Steele. We can make it work."

Just then, the crowd erupted, and the ring bell declared that the tag match had ended. It was time for the main event.

CHAPTER TWENTY-FOUR

Tony's perpetually bulging eyes swelled to their breaking point. "Wait here." He took off down the hallway with all the athletic coordination of a three-legged hamster.

"Great promo, Mommy," Addie said. "Didn't know you were such a good liar."

"Learned it from your NiNi."

"Are you sure this is going to work, Sebastian?" Bennett asked.

"Of course it's going to work. I thought of it, didn't I?"

"That's what worries us," Addie said.

"Ye of little faith. I am a catch wrestling expert and possess a wide-ranging arsenal of painful submission holds, from wrist locks to toe holds and neck cranks. Once we're all in the ring together, I'll simply stretch the truth out of them. Granted, it is somewhat beneath me to resort to such base physicality, but even the smartest, cleverest, most handsome detectives must be willing to get their hands dirty on occasion. It's all part of the job."

"Good thing humility isn't," Addie and Bennett's mom said.

"Oh, it is, but I am far too humble to bring up my staggering humility."

Two chubby, unathletic men in camouflage pants and pizza-stained tank tops staggered through the backstage curtain, each favoring an injured leg and leaning on one another for support. As soon as the curtain closed, they straightened up and started walking normally back to the dressing room. They gave the Tres Terrores dirty looks on the way past.

"Those are the Grave Stompers," Addie whispered to Sebastian. "Tiny brought them in from Detroit to put over the Hicksons."

"They should try putting over a salad sometime."

The Stompers stopped short of the dressing room door and stepped aside to let out Tony, Mad Mike Dean, Vince Manero, and Lenny Lambda. Tony, now carrying both the briefcase and the KCW Heavyweight Championship belt, congratulated the Stompers on a great match and then provided hasty introductions to his newest business partners.

"These are the Tres Terrores. And you'll be working with El Mono Diablo here. The finish stays the same. Lenny goes over. You guys can figure out the rest. Gotta go." Before Tony could get away, Sebastian handed him something. At first, Tony seemed confused, but he quickly caught the meaning and was on his way.

Tony was barely through the curtain when the jubilant Hickson Brothers appeared in their ludicrous ring attire, which consisted of shimmery headbands, multi-colored arm tassels, and paisley-patterned bell bottoms. They had the tag team titles on their shoulders.

"How'd we do, Lenny?" Ronnie Hickson asked the moment he saw his idol and mentor.

Lenny, already in full character, had his sunglasses on and his hair hanging in his face like frosted linguine. He wore a black leather jacket over plain black trunks and boots, conveying his no-nonsense attitude and toughness. Such artful details really rounded out his performance and almost made people forget he couldn't win a fight to save his life. He removed the toothpick from his mouth and gave them a two-word review in his gruff stage voice. "Killed it."

The Hickson Brothers high-fived.

"We're gonna go clean up," Ronnie Hickson said, "but we'll be out there to help you celebrate after you beat these jabronis."

Ricky Hickson nodded to the Tres Terrores. "Who's the circus act?"

"Tony made a deal with a Mexican promotion," Lambda said through clenched teeth. "It's a fatal four-way now."

"Gonna make the win even sweeter," Ronnie Hickson said. "You're goin' down, little Mexicos."

The Hicksons wished Lenny good luck and continued to mock the Tres Terrores on their way to the dressing room until Addie lunged at them, sending them scurrying for safety.

Manero approached Addie and Bennett's mother. He was stuffed into red leather pants, the waist of which was hidden by his flabby gut. He was also drenched in enough baby oil to float a battleship, but it still couldn't bring out his nonexistent muscles. Instead, he just looked like an engorged sausage about to be deep fried.

"They speak English?"

"A little," she said.

"Good. We'll call it in the ring." Manero winked at her. "And maybe I'll call you out of the ring." He tried to post his oil-slicked hand on the wall next to her only to have it slide sideways. Thankfully, he steadied himself before falling and splitting his pants. He played it off by moonwalking away and shooting finger guns at her.

Dean, dressed in the same work shirt and blue jeans he typically wore on plumbing jobs, finished wrapping white athletic tape around his wrists and hands. He tossed the empty roll over his shoulder and lumbered up to Sebastian. "What's your finish, kid?"

"Voltereta de mono."

"Huh?"

Addie and Bennett's mother provided translation. "Monkey flip."

"Cool," Dean said. "I'll kick out."

The bingo hall's PA system blared Manero's theme music, an ear-punishing hard rock song that he had composed himself. The crowd seemed to like it and even sang along. Next out was Dean, whose "music" was just a chainsaw over people screaming. An obnoxious techno track played Lambda to the ring.

The Tres Terrores took their places at the curtain, Sebastian in the middle, Addie and Bennett on his wings, and their mother bringing up the rear. They listened to Tony explain the new addition to the main event.

Sebastian took a deep breath. "It's go time."

"We should have brought music," Addie said.

"I did."

"Monkey, so help me…."

Tony screamed, "El Mono Diablo!" And then the opening notes of *Baby Elephant Walk* filled the air.

Sebastian never heard Addie's mumbled promise of retribution because he was already through the curtain, flaring his cape like a glittering sail. Bennett was delighted with the musical choice, and it provided him with a much needed boost of confidence for the walk to the ring. Addie's natural wrestling instincts took over, and she immediately started working heel. She shouted insults, threatened people with her cast, and made several rude gestures until her mother put a halt to her antics. Despite Addie's best efforts, the crowd greeted the Tres Terrores with confused silence. Sebastian didn't seem to mind. He paraded around the ring at a snail's clip—arms outstretched, cape flowing—and basked in the spotlight. Dean was certainly not amused, and he leaned over the top rope and expressed his distaste for Sebastian's leisurely entrance with a stream of vile obscenities. It did nothing to accelerate Sebastian's pace.

When he finally did get in the ring, Sebastian made a point to climb the turnbuckles in each corner and salute the crowd with raised fists. No one cheered. All the while, the referee and Lambda did their best to hold back Dean. Sebastian remained oblivious to their efforts.

The music cut, and the announcer at ringside began the introductions. Sebastian removed his cape and handed it through the ropes to Bennett.

"Good luck, Sebastian."

"I'm not the one who's going to need it." He jogged in place to warm up. "Can't imagine this will take long. Think I'll start with Dean."

"Might want to stay away from him," Addie said. "Pretty sure he wants to kill you."

"Please. Like I'm scared of that overgrown infant."

Sebastian heard his name announced and strutted to the center of the ring, where he proceeded to place his hands on his head and swivel his hips. Stunned silence. Tony raised the KCW Heavyweight Championship one last time and then exited the ring. He invited Addie and Bennett's mother to join him at the timekeeper's table, and he even let her hold the championship belt so he could keep hugging his briefcase full of cash. The other Tres Terrores worked Sebastian's corner.

The bell sounded.

Most fatal four-way matches typically start slow, with the competitors hesitant to make the first move. Often, the wrestlers will pair up and wage two separate clashes. However, on this night, the echo of the bell was still being heard when Dean, Manero, and Lambda all jumped Sebastian and began pummeling him with kicks and punches. The beating lasted much longer than necessary, and the crowd cheered louder with each successive blow. Satisfied Sebastian was little more than a puddle of soup on the mat, Dean, Manero, and Lambda left him for dead in the corner and began working their intended three-way match.

Sebastian crawled to the ropes and stared at Addie and Bennett with glassy eyes. "Did they tap yet?"

"Monkey, you're gonna have to do more than head-butt their fists," Addie said.

"Go after Manero," Bennett said. "He's old."

"Good thinking." Sebastian pried himself off the mat and adjusted his dislodged mask. "Once more into the fray."

Dean had been thrown from the ring, leaving Manero and Lambda trading forearms. Sebastian vaulted onto Manero's back and attempted to sink in a sleeper hold only to slide down his baby-oiled body like a greased maypole. Manero gave Lambda one final forearm smash and then heaved Sebastian high in the air and delivered a devastating powerbomb. A flying knee from Lambda to Manero's chin prevented a pin attempt, and while the two of them reengaged with a returning Dean, Sebastian slowly rolled his way back to his corner.

"You okay, Sebastian?" Bennett asked.

"All part of the plan. Just letting the heels get some heat before making my dramatic comeback."

Addie said, "So you're not the worst wrestler I've ever seen, you're just selling?"

"Yep, just selling." Sebastian used the ropes to pull himself up. "But now might be the perfect time for some aerial offense."

"You sure as heck can't wrestle on the ground, might as well try the air."

"Prepare to witness the unrivaled talent of El Mono Diablo, the greatest high-flyer in all of Mexico."

Sebastian climbed the turnbuckles and steadied himself on the top rope. He waited until he saw an opening, and then he soared through the air for a beautiful cross-body to an unsuspecting Dean. Sadly, Lambda intercepted him with a running dropkick to the gut, sending Sebastian crashing back into the turnbuckles. He crumpled to the mat like a used tissue.

Sebastian could barely lift his head. "Oh, look. Steve Thacker's in the front row. Wonder how many stars I'll get. I'm seeing at least a dozen at the moment."

While Bennett tried to revive Sebastian, Addie went to the timekeeper's table to consult with her mother.

"Monkey's hopeless." She had to shout to be heard over the raucous crowd. "We're gonna need a Plan B."

"Like what?"

Addie snatched the championship belt off her mother's lap. "Maybe he can hit 'em with this." That's when she noticed something peculiar. The white leather on the inside of the belt was pristine. "Wait a minute…." She checked the front of the belt again to make sure it was the same one recovered from their backyard. "Hey, Tiny."

Tony, still clutching the briefcase to his chest, was so engrossed in the match that he didn't hear her, so she banged her cast off the table a few times to get his attention.

"Did you clean the belt?"

"Wow, Ladrona, your English is really good."

Addie smacked the table again with her cast. "Focus, Tiny! Did you clean the belt?"

"Yeah, of course. I had the plates polished to make it look nice for the new champ."

"But you didn't remove any writing from the inside of the belt?"

"What are you talking about? I don't know how you do things in Mexico, but no one would ever disrespect the KCW title like that."

Addie returned the championship to her mother and sprinted back to Sebastian's corner. She jumped up and down and waved her arms over her head. "We gotta get Monkey's attention."

"What's wrong?" Bennett asked.

"I found a clue."

Bennett joined in on the arm waving, but Sebastian was far too busy to notice. He was currently stretched across Dean's shoulders and being spun into delirium. After enduring a nauseating number of rotations and getting slammed to the canvas, Sebastian tried to stand, stumbled around in a circle a few times, and then ate a shoulder block from Lambda that sent him tumbling into the corner.

"Good, you saw us," Addie said. "That's not the real belt."

Sebastian sat back against the turnbuckle and braced his arms along the bottom rope. His head lulled from side to side. "I can taste colors."

"Snap out of it, Monkey. Did you hear what I said? That's not the real belt."

"What do you mean?" Bennett asked.

"Remember the night Mitch beat Daddy and started the fight in the dressing room? When no one was looking, I wrote something on the inside of the belt."

Sebastian started to come around. "What did you write?"

"Cat butt."

"Why would you write cat butt on the inside of the belt?"

"Because Mitch was a cat butt. And every time he looked at the belt, I wanted him to be reminded that he was, in fact, a cat butt."

"Makes sense."

"That belt over there, the one they got out of our backyard, doesn't say cat butt."

"It's not the real belt?" Bennett said.

"That's what I've been trying to tell you."

"But why would the killer plant a fake championship belt in our yard? Why not just use the real one that he stole from Mitch?"

"I don't know, maybe he lost it?"

Sebastian struggled to stand. "Or maybe he didn't want to lose it." He limped over to Dean, who had just planted Manero with a DDT. "Mike, old sport. How about you and I do a crowd spot? We could—"

Dean pressed Sebastian over his head and lobbed him into the crowd. The fans went crazy. They were so excited, they didn't even bother catching Sebastian. He bounced a few times and ended up somewhere around the third row.

The more charitable spectators helped Sebastian up and shoved him back toward the ring. He weaved and wobbled, selling the all-too-real injuries, until he reached a certain fan in the front row. Without warning, Sebastian cupped the man behind the head, planted his feet on the man's hips, and then fell backward and kicked with all his chimpanzee might, flipping the man over the ropes and into the ring. The flying fan brought the match to a screeching halt. But it wasn't just any fan. It was Steve Thacker.

Sebastian called for the bell, which Addie and Bennett's mother obliged, and requested the ring announcer's microphone. He tapped it a few times to make sure it was on.

"Steve Thacker, while you lie there, hopefully as uncomfortable as you can be, I want you to listen to me." Sebastian rolled under the bottom rope to get in the ring. "But before we go any further, I must reveal my true identify. For I am not El Mono Diablo, the pride of Mexican wrestling." He pulled off his luchador mask and smiled, confident that the crowd would recognize him. And someone did.

Tony sprung from his seat. "Gary Carl?"

"Yes, it is I, Sebastian Winthrop, chimp detective. Please hold your applause. I stand before you today to declare that Mitch Mayhem's true killer is none other than the Squared Circle's own Steve Thacker. That's right, the same man who made a career of ruining wrestling, all while murdering sentence structures and the accepted rules of grammar, also killed one of its brightest stars."

The crowd gasped.

Like everyone in attendance, the other wrestlers in the ring seemed uncertain what to make of these accusations. Manero spoke for everyone when he said, "Is that true, Steve?"

A defiant Thacker stood tall in his acid-washed jeans and tucked-in Japanese wrestling T-shirt. "Of course not. Why would I want to kill Mitch?"

"Because Mitch didn't wrestle your preferred style," Sebastian said. "He was a throwback to a time when charisma and storytelling ruled the day, not the endless high spots and no selling that you've popularized. Seeing Mitch as champion ate you up inside. He was a living testament to your ignorance, a shining example that you had no idea what you were talking about. But it wasn't always that way. You championed Mitch in his younger days, giving him award after award. But during his time away from wrestling, your ego grew. You were no longer content reporting on the shows. You wanted to be the show. Sure, you'd never be able to survive working in the wrestling industry, but you could certainly critique and belittle those who did. Why couldn't people see that you were always right and that all those stupid promoters and performers were wrong? Then along came Lenny Lambda and the Hickson Brothers, three upstarts who appealed to a younger generation of fans. Old-timers hated them, claiming they were killing the business. But what did they know? They didn't have your vision, your knowledge of what wrestling should be. You latched on to Lambda and the Hicksons like the parasitic virus you are, hailing them as the best workers in wrestling. Every match was five stars. Some even got six or seven stars. You were finally one of the cool kids."

"Hey," Lambda said in his gruff, gravelly voice, "I am the best, and all my matches are instant classics."

"Yeah, according to one looney old man. But you weren't even the champ. Mitch was. And that was a big problem for you, wasn't it, Steve? Lenny had to be the champion. That was the only way you'd be proven right, that your genius would be recognized. But as long as Mitch was alive, your darling Lenny Lambda would never win the title. Worse yet, on the night he was murdered, Mitch stood in this very ring and called you out for your lies. You were eager to report those bogus stories Manero was feeding you about Mitch. Anything to make him look bad."

"Hey, little buddy," Manero said. "Keep me out of this. I'm no stooge for the dirt sheets."

Addie shouted from ringside, "You're the stoogiest stooge who ever stooged!"

"And Mitch knew it," Sebastian said. "He refused to work with you and buried you in that same promo. But Steve here was the one truly offended. How dare he question you, the leading influencer in wrestling, the man who had given him so many prestigious awards. You went to his house that night to confront him. But Bonecrusher was already there. You waited for him to leave, and then you made your move. Mitch invited you inside. Things got heated. And you killed him."

"I didn't do it," Thacker said. "Bonecrusher killed Mitch. They found the championship belt in his backyard."

"Correction," Sebastian said. "They found *a* championship belt, not *the* championship belt. Unbeknownst to you, Bonecrusher's daughter had marked the real championship with a hidden message for Mitch. The belt buried in Bonecrusher's backyard, that same belt right over there, does not have that message. Thus, that belt is a fake. Why would the killer keep the real belt and replace it with a fake? Because the killer is a wrestling historian, a collector of memorabilia. When my associates and I interviewed you in your apartment, we commented on the many championships you had displayed. And do you remember what you told us? You said they were just replicas. You had the real belts safely locked away. That same collection is where we will find the true KCW Heavyweight Championship, the one you stole from Mitch on the night you murdered him. You tried to use the replica belt to seal Bonecrusher's conviction. But in the end, it was that same belt that was your undoing. You should have booked a better finish."

For the first time that evening, the crowd cheered Sebastian. He waved appreciation and bowed before continuing.

"Yes, Steve Thacker, you are guilty of murder, but that is hardly your only crime. You've warped minds and darkened souls. You've created a generation of intolerable wrestling fans, smart marks who trash anything that strays from their fantasy bookings. Naïve, witless morons too dumb to recognize they're killing the very thing they claim to love."

Mumbled protests bubbled up from the crowd. Addie spun on the disgruntled masses. "Touch grass, nerds. You know it's true. Preach, Monkey!"

"Know what else is true?" Sebastian said. "Steve Thacker's reign of terror has ended. The king of smarks has fallen. May another never rise again."

"You think you're so smart," Thacker said, each word dipped in venom. "But you don't understand wrestling like I do. Nobody does. Why can't you see how wrong you all are? Am I the only sane person here?"

"It's okay, Steve," Lambda said in his normal, nonperforming voice. "I understand. Others understand. We can get you the help you need."

"No." Demonic hellfire animated Thacker's aged eyes, and his tongue flopped loose from a sinister sneer. "This isn't over. It's just time for the swerve ending."

With remarkable speed and agility, the elderly Thacker choke-slammed Manero and then wrecked Dean with a running spear. He used the momentum to roll toward Lenny, where he effortlessly regained his feet, mouthed "I love you," and blasted him in the chin with a superkick. The Hickson Brothers hit the ring to defend Lenny and met a similar fate, each superkicked into oblivion.

"Whoa," Sebastian said. "Did not see that coming."

"Get him, Monkey!" Addie yelled.

"You can do it, Sebastian!" Bennett shouted.

Sebastian slowly lowered the microphone to the canvas, trying to avoid any sudden movements that might trigger the madman. "Okay, if that's how you want it." He put up his dukes in a classic Queensberry boxing posture. "Let's dance."

Thacker screamed like a banshee and blitzed Sebastian only to perform an exquisite tope con hilo, leaping over both the chimp detective and the top rope, somersaulting in midair, and landing in full sprint without ever breaking stride. A relieved Sebastian collapsed against the ropes and wiped the sweat from his eyes. "Oh, thank God."

Whether they feared the crazed newsletter writer or simply believed it was all part of the show, not a single fan attempted to stop Thacker's escape. He was mere feet from the bingo hall exit when justice finally arrived in the form of a vicious clothesline that folded him like a cheap suit. The crowd popped big for the ferocious assault, and when Sebastian, Addie, Bennett, and their mother reached the scene, they found a familiar face standing over Thacker.

"NiNi!" yelled Addie and Bennett.

Sebastian smiled at his Amazonian queen. "Didn't think you were going to make it."

"I wouldn't have missed this for the world." She gave Thacker a stiff kick to keep him down. "And I brought friends."

Chief Bouchard and Detective Carter came hustling into view. They had been stationed at the other exits.

"We heard everything, Sebastian," Detective Carter said. "Looks like you solved another one." He hauled the still woozy Thacker to his feet.

"All in a day's work, Raymond. Someone must protect the good citizens of this fair town. Chief Bouchard, I trust you will see to it that Stanley Pajakowski is released posthaste. Would hate for your grievous mistake to last a moment longer than necessary."

Chief Bouchard poked a pudgy Canadian finger at his primate adversary. "Look here, Monkey. It's no secret that I hate you."

"But…you respect me."

"No, I hate you. That's it."

The chief secured Thacker by the arm and held him steady while Detective Carter handcuffed him. All the jostling brought Thacker back to coherence. "That's right, I killed Mitch. I'd do it again too. He deserved it, just like all you wrestling infidels deserve it. And I would have gotten away with it if it wasn't for that stupid monkey."

Addie ran up to the restrained Thacker and kicked him in the shin. "He's not a monkey, he's a chimpanzee." She slung her arm around Sebastian's shoulders. "And he's my friend."

"I want her arrested!" Thacker cried, favoring his wounded leg. "You saw what she did. You all saw it."

"I didn't see anything," Detective Carter said. "How about you, Chief?"

Chief Bouchard pushed his tuque up a bit higher on his forehead. "Sorry. Honest, I didn't see it. I'm pretty terrible at noticing things like that. Guess that's why I'm not a better cop. But, c'mon, it's almost time for *Trailer Park Boys*."

Chief Bouchard and Detective Carter dragged Thacker outside to a waiting squad car. The fans in attendance also started to leave, with many debating the merits of ending a championship match via disqualification. Tony congratulated Sebastian on catching Mitch's real killer, and he was shocked to learn that Ladrona and Bandito were actually Addie and Bennett. He told them that he couldn't wait to see their dad back in the ring. In fact, he was going to use the whole 'wrongly accused of murder' storyline to push Bonecrusher to the top. But he did have one important question.

"I guess this means you really aren't representing a Mexican promotion, huh?"

Michelle shook her head. "I'm their mother. We've actually met before. I used to come to all of Stan's matches."

"No streaming TV deal either?"

"Sadly, no."

"Do I get to keep the money?"

"Actually," Sebastian said, "now that you mention it, I probably could just invest in the promotion. I mean, what else am I going to do with a paltry fifty grand?"

Tony nearly jumped out of his socks. "Really? That would be amazing."

"I'm still selling Pioneer Scout cookies," Addie said in way of suggestion.

After a moment's thought, Sebastian slowly reached over and took the briefcase from Tony. "Yeah, I'm going to need this back."

"Tony!" Jill Johnson ran up and hugged him. "That ending was so good. Did you book it yourself?"

"Oh, yeah, of course. All my idea."

"That's the sort of creative my character needs. I've been working on some stuff. Maybe we can workshop it together. Cool if I call you tomorrow?"

"Absolutely."

Tony watched her walk away for three whole seconds before fainting. Michelle stepped over him to get to her mother.

"I'm sorry I got so crazy about everything."

"It's okay," NiNi said. "I'm sorry that I didn't tell you about us investigating the case. You had a right to know."

"Your heart was in the right place. And I guess it usually is."

Mother and daughter hugged.

"Let's get out of here," NiNi said. "I think we have someone to pick up from jail."

The Pajakowski family and the great chimp detective walked out of the bingo hall together, united once more. Addie still had her arm around Sebastian.

"About that friend stuff," he said. "Always thought of us as more like professional acquaintances."

"We're friends."

"Would you believe friendly associates?"

"Nope. We're friends, Monkey. Deal with it."

CHAPTER TWENTY-FIVE

The bright yellow house at the top of Mulberry Hill, once shuttered and dark, was now filled with life. The lawn had been manicured, the bushes sculpted. Water shot majestically from the circular driveway's center fountain. Sunlight poured through the crystal-clear windows, bathing the previously locked, musty rooms in radiance. All the floors had been mopped, vacuumed, or scrubbed. Fixtures polished. Furniture uncovered. Not a speck of dust marred the pristine palace. The revitalization required an army of professional cleaners working around the clock, but Sebastian spared no expense in preparing to host his honored guests.

NiNi and the Pajakowskis arrived for dinner wearing their Sunday best. Sebastian, who was in his customary smoking jacket and stylish khakis, had planned to fly in an executive chef from New York to cook the meal, but NiNi convinced him to just have things catered by the Steel Trolley Diner. He acquiesced, partly to make Addie and Bennett happy, but mainly to get some more of that surprisingly delicious banana cream pie. After dinner, they retired to the sitting room, an airy oasis of whites and pale yellows that also featured an ivory grand piano. Sebastian could only play one song, and Addie knew exactly what it was and refused to let him do it. Instead, he clicked a button on a special remote control, and one of the walls turned into a giant TV screen equipped with every gaming system imaginable. While Addie and Bennett excitedly explored the possibilities, Stanley Pajakowski couldn't stop expressing his gratitude.

"Thought I'd never have another one of these nights with my family," he said. "Can't thank you enough, Sebastian. You saved my life."

"It was a life worth saving."

"Still can't believe Thacker was the killer."

"Did you ever find out if he was the one driving the van?" NiNi asked. She looked stunning in an off-the-shoulder peasant blouse and ankle-length skirt, and Sebastian made sure to tell her as much every chance he got.

"He came clean about everything," Sebastian said. "Didn't want to use his own car to tail us, so he went out of town to rent the van."

"You should get vehicular assault added to the charges," Michelle said. "He shouldn't get away with trying to run down my kids."

"And your mother," NiNi reminded.

"Oh, yeah, that too."

"I'm just glad things are back to normal," Stanley said. "Hopefully I can get my job back at the garage, and it'll be like none of this ever happened."

"About that," Sebastian said. "How would you like to come work for me?"

"What do you mean?"

"After serious consideration, I have decided to resume my detective career. I could use a good man like yourself to keep my fleet of cars running or to just help maintain the property. You could be the Kato to my Green Hornet."

"You have a fleet of cars?"

"Yeah," Addie said from across the room. "A bunch of cool ones too. But he only drives a dopey hatchback that's like older than NiNi."

Stanley looked to his wife. "What do you think?"

"There would be a position for you as well," Sebastian said. "If I'm working cases again, I will need an executive assistant. And when you complete your studies, you could even be my legal counsel. I will start you each off at twice your current salaries, and there will be opportunities for advancement and pay raises as we go. You will find I am a benevolent boss."

"Twice as much?" Michelle said. "That will certainly make paying the mortgage easier."

"That brings me to my next point." Sebastian clasped his hands behind his back. "If this experience has taught me anything, it's that no chimp is an island. I've spent far too much time alone these past few years. The only real growth comes from change. My life needs changing. Sure, I've already started wearing denim and eating diner food, but that's not enough. I must continue to grow, change, evolve. I wish to be part of something bigger than myself. With that in mind, I am formally inviting you to make this your home as well."

"You want us to live here?" Michelle said, looking around at her opulent surroundings. "In this mansion? With you?"

Addie and Bennett overheard the negotiations and abandoned their game to get in on the action.

"Are you serious?" Stanley said.

"This house is entirely too big for me. You guys could have the east wing. I prefer the west simply because it's a little farther from Philadelphia. I will cover all utilities, property taxes, and the like. And I've obviously grown quite found of at least one of your children."

Bennett raised his hand. "I vote to live with Sebastian."

"Me too," Addie said. "Did you see the size of that TV?"

"I don't know," Michelle said. "This all sounds too good to be true. What do you think, Mom?"

"I think Sebastian is not only kind and generous but remarkably brave. Aside from all the wonderful things he would be doing for you, think of how much you could enrich his life. Seems like a beautiful opportunity for mutual growth. You'll be good for each other. And that TV is, like, so big."

"Thank you, my dear," Sebastian said. He kissed NiNi's hand. "There's always room for one more."

"I appreciate the offer, but I like my house. I think I'll stay where I am." She winked at him. "But I'm sure we'll still be seeing plenty of each other."

Sebastian clutched at his heart as if struck by Cupid's arrow, and then he turned and started fielding questions from Addie and Bennett about the house's notable amenities. Michelle took the chance to have a whispered exchange with her mother.

"You shouldn't encourage him."

"Oh, he's harmless."

"He's a monkey."

"Dating is hard at my age. And let's be honest, I've done worse."

With Addie and Bennett badgering him to see the mysterious underground floors above the garage, Sebastian looked to their parents and asked an important question. "Is it official?"

Stanley checked with Michelle for final confirmation. She stood and gathered the kids around them for a family huddle. There was a brief, hushed debate, and then the Pajakowskis turned to face Sebastian.

"Looks like it's official," Stanley said.

Sebastian shook his hand. "Welcome to your new home."

"Welcome to your new family," Addie said. She opened her arms wide for a big hug.

Sebastian considered the invitation. "The handshake is fine."

"Monkey!"

ACKNOWLEDGEMENTS

A special thanks to all the wrestling stars and personalities who provided inspiration, particularly CM Punk and Jim Cornette. A significant debt of gratitude is also owed to such pioneering chimps as Fred J. Muggs, Zippy the Wonder Chimp, and Lancelot Link.

ABOUT THE AUTHOR

Michael Dell is a mystery writer, hockey blogger, and independent researcher who is obsessed with hidden truths. The son of a police detective, Michael grew up in Western Pennsylvania wanting to fight crime, but thin bones and a general dislike for the sight of his own blood made it far safer to stay home and memorize *Columbo* episodes. In 2014, he earned an MFA in Writing Popular Fiction from Seton Hill University. When not chronicling the adventures of Honest John Churchfield or Sebastian Winthrop, he enjoys recording fake radio shows, reading old comic books, and watching ridiculous amounts of professional wrestling. He hopes to one day find a box of money.

CONTACT

Mailing List: list.oneninebooks.com

Join my mailing list to receive a free Honest John Churchfield short story. The list will feature Churchfield and Sebastian Winthrop updates, personal news, writing and editing tips, book recommendations, author interviews, and probably a bunch of chimp pics.

Email: Dell@OneNineBooks.com

X: @OneNineBooks

And if you liked *Monkey Flip*, please consider reviewing it on Amazon. Every little bit helps. Thank you!